5.6

MOUNTAIN MIRACLE

BOOK 6

MOUNTAIN MIRACLE

T. L. TEDROW

THOMAS NELSON PUBLISHERS
Nashville

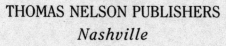

Published in Nashville, Tennessee, by Thomas Nelson, Inc., and distributed in Canada by Lawson Falle, Ltd., Cambridge, Ontario.

Scripture quotations are from the KING JAMES VERSION of the Bible.

Library of Congress Cataloging-in-Publication Data

Tedrow, Thomas L.
    Mountain miracle / [T.L. Tedrow].
      p. cm. — (The Days of Laura Ingalls Wilder ; bk. 6)
    Summary: As she gets to know and like the reclusive woman healer whom some in town consider a witch, Laura realizes that Mansfield, Missouri, faces a much greater threat from a self-proclaimed religious leader.
    ISBN 0-8407-7733-7
    I. Wilder, Laura Ingalls, 1867–1957—Juvenile fiction. [1. Wilder, Laura Ingalls, 1867–1957—Fiction. 2. Frontier and pioneer life—Missouri—Fiction. 3. Witchcraft—Fiction. 4. Missouri—Fiction.] I. Title. II. Series: Tedrow, Thomas L. Days of Laura Ingalls Wilder ; bk. 6
PZ7.T227Mo   1992
[Fic]—dc20   92-19927
                                                CIP
                                                AC

Printed in the United States of America

1 2 3 4 5 6 7 - 96 95 94 93 92

Dedicated To

*Sam Moore, who has shown me that faith and
determination can move mountains.*

*And to Carla, my wife, best friend, and co-author.
When the chips were down, she picked them up and
we started again.*

And Special Thanks To

*My four children, C. T., Tyler, Tara, and Travis,
who inspire and help with what I write.*

*My mother, Gertrude Tedrow, who
taught me faith, courage, kindness, love, and understanding.*

*My late father, Richard Tedrow, who told me I could be
anything I wanted. I miss him every day.*

*My sister, Carol Newman, and brother, Richard Tedrow,
good friends and good family.*

17,006

CONTENTS

FOREWORD

Laura Ingalls Wilder is loved the world over for her pioneer books and the wonderful television series that was based on them. Though much has been written about the Old West, it was Laura Ingalls Wilder who brought the frontier to life for millions of young readers.

The Laura Ingalls Wilder story did not stop after her last book. She and her husband, Manly, and daughter, Rose, moved to Mansfield, Missouri, from South Dakota in 1894. Laura was twenty-seven, Manly thirty-eight, and Rose was seven. They arrived with only one hundred dollars and the few possessions they had salvaged from their house that had burned down. They used the money as a down payment on a broken-down farm, and after a decade of hard work, they had built Apple Hill Farm, the finest house Laura had ever lived in!

Laura Ingalls Wilder went on to become a pioneer journalist in Mansfield, where for sixteen years she was a columnist for the farm family weekly, *Missouri Ruralist*. She spoke her mind about the environment and land abuse; preached women's rights; lamented the consequences of war; and observed the march of progress as cars, planes, radios, and new inventions changed America forever.

In *Mountain Miracle*, book six in our series The Days of Laura Ingalls Wilder, Laura confronts the consequences of prejudice and superstition. What is strange and different to some is normal to others, a fact relevant to problems we face even today.

While this book is a fictional account of Laura's exploits, it

CHAPTER 1

OZARK CALL OF THE WILD

The sound of rattling antlers echoed across the ridge from Apple Hill Farm. It seemed to accent the dusk that was settling over the Ozarks.

Laura Ingalls Wilder turned her head toward the Ozark call of the wild. From her "thinking rock"—the boulder on top of the ridge where she sat to reflect on her life and problems—Laura looked out, hoping to catch sight of the bucks locking horns.

The rugged Missouri land that surrounded Apple Hill Farm was like a zoo without fences. The strict no-hunting policy on the hundreds of acres that Laura and her husband, Manly, had scrimped and struggled to buy gave the animals safe refuge. The birds repaid the kindness by keeping their orchards and gardens pest-free. By working in harmony with nature, Apple Hill Farm fruit was grown without pesticides and was considered the finest in the Ozarks.

It hadn't been that way at first. Laura had grown up on the prairie eating freshly killed game. When she and her family arrived in Missouri, they'd survived off the animals in the hills. But their attitudes changed as the farm grew. They could afford store-bought meat and raised their own chickens, sheep, and cattle. It just came naturally to leave the wild animals on their land alone.

Laura heard the sound again. On the other side of the ravine, a white-tail buck was moving silently across the top of the adjoining ridge. With the sunset framing him, it was a sight Laura concentrated on, hoping never to forget this picture of nature's beauty.

He has heard it too, she thought. *He knows there's a doe somewhere the other bucks are fighting over.*

Laura decided to follow behind the buck as best she could. Taking the ridge trail into the ravine, she carefully made her way to the other side. She could still hear the sounds of deers rattling their antlers together, but had lost track of the buck. So she followed the sounds, hoping to catch up with him before it got too dark.

She again caught sight of the majestic animal about a hundred yards beyond. Like her father, Pa Ingalls, had taught her, Laura kept out of sight, following behind, low to the ground.

A wild turkey crossed the deer's path and a group of chattering squirrels ran alongside. Nothing seemed to sway the buck as he cocked his head back and forth, using the sound of the antlers to guide him.

Laura watched as he sniffed the ground for signs of a passing doe. *Maybe he thinks he'll get to the doe while the others are fighting,* she laughed to herself. When the buck stopped, she hid behind a fallen tree to watch and wait.

The buck was positioned by the base of a big oak tree, scratching his eight-point antler crown against the bark. As the bark snapped loose, he butted against the tree in a show of strength to the other bucks he hadn't seen yet.

Laura smiled at the drama of nature playing out before her. Males fighting over females. No matter what the species, the instinct was there. The bucks were fighting for the attention of the doe, who was probably hiding in the bushes to see which of the bucks would stand his ground.

The buck sparred with the bushes around the oak, waiting for his challengers to come forward. He knocked off the new leaves and lifted a bush which tangled in his antlers. Dirt flew everywhere as he shook his head back and forth, trying to throw off the maze of roots.

Laura heard the rattling antlers again and looked around for the first sign of the doe. With the bucks fighting so close, she knew that the doe was also nearby, waiting for the outcome.

Click.

Laura's smile faded at the sound. She looked around frantically, now knowing what was going on.

Click . . . click.

It was the sound of a rifle cocking! The sound of the antlers was a hunter's trick! The buck was being called to his death!

She looked at the beautiful buck and frantically tried to find the hunter. The majestic animal tilted his head and grunted into the air, calling out his intention to breed.

Laura peered through the twilight. *Where is the hunter?*

The buck spun around. Laura knew that a shot would ring out any second.

Who is hunting on my property? She looked around, trying to find where the hunter was hiding. *Is he behind that bush? Is he over by the rocks? No . . . wait . . . there he is. Up in the big oak tree.*

Laura saw the camouflaged hunter hidden in the crook of the branches. Dressed in a brown, rough-cloth coat, only his thick reddish moustache stood out against the brown and green of the forest.

The hunter adjusted his position, using his stockinged feet to brace himself. He had taken off his boots to keep the noise down.

He's drawing a bead on the deer. An easy shot. The deer will drop before he hears the shot.

Laura was speechless, wanting to stop the hunter, but caught up in the fear of the moment. She tried to scream, but couldn't.

Crack! The branch under the hunter's foot broke loose. He cursed softly, trying to keep from falling, but the buck had heard it.

Muscles tense, ears up, the buck tried to smell the direction of the danger.

Laura stood up. The hunter braced himself on the branch. With his gun cradled, he picked up the brace of antlers that hung above him and rubbed them together to trick the buck again.

That was the sound that Laura and the buck had heard. The sound of bucks fighting over a doe. The sound that triggered the urge to breed inside the buck. The sound of death.

The hunter aimed again. He drew down on the buck, sure of his shot.

Laura waved her arms to warn the deer. The buck's ears perked and turned toward Laura, ready to jump and run. The hunter adjusted his aim and smiled, not noticing Laura.

Then she saw it. Just as the hunter squeezed off his shot, a rock hit him on the shoulder.

Kaboom! The shot went wide and echoed over the Ozarks as the buck spooked and raced away.

"Don't hunt 'round here. I've warned you before," came an old woman's voice from somewhere up ahead.

The hunter was furious. "You old witch! You got no right to stop me from hunting for the Flock."

Laura caught sight of the old woman. It was Josie, the herb woman. From chin to forehead, her face was a solid wrinkle. Ugly warts with thick black hairs stuck out at odd angles from her chin. Some called her a witch and some called her a miracle worker.

She was a mountain wallflower who'd never married and still lived alone in the same cabin she was raised in. Hidden away in the hollow, two ridges over, no road led to her house, and only those who had business with Josie ever went there.

Josie put down her basket and stood below the oak, shaking her fist. "Come down here, you trespassin' thief!" she screamed, waving his hunting boots around in the air.

"Get outta here, evil woman!" the hunter screamed back.

Josie banged her gnarled, carved cane against the tree. "I said, come down here 'fore I come up and get you!"

"You don't got your broom with you," the man snapped.

Josie cackled. "Broom? I don't need my broom to come up and drag you down."

The hunter began descending carefully. Josie screamed up, "What's your name?"

"I am Brother Bill," he said in a surly voice.

"You're one of them snake handlers, ain't ya?" she asked in a sneering tone.

Brother Bill nodded. "I am of the Flock."

Laura crept forward as Josie cackled. "Flock? More like a bunch of sidewinders if you ask me."

Sitting on the branch above her, the hunter hesitated coming the rest of the way down. "Jackson Rutherford had a vision and told me to bring him a deer."

"He been eatin' locoweed again?" the old woman laughed.

The hunter spit down near Josie, then dropped to the ground, glaring at her coldly. "Rutherford is a special man—sent to lead us through his visions."

Josie spit on the same spot and backed him against the tree with her cane. "You tell your Jackson Rutherford next time he has a vision, to get his tail down to the butcher shop. No hunter's gonna kill my animal friends."

Bill chuckled. "Maybe someday I'll mistake your old bones as bein' a deer and—"

Laura walked up and interrupted. "—and maybe you'll be put in jail."

"Who are you?" the hunter asked.

Josie smiled and winked at Laura. "I got me a witness now, who owns the next land over."

"You're the rich one, the writer," Bill said. "Rutherford has had a vision about you and your land."

"Oh, and what was that?" Laura asked.

"You are not of the Flock. You have no need to know."

Josie pushed him with her cane. "Time for you to git on outta here," she laughed, waving his boots in the air.

The hunter glared. "Give me my boots back."

"They're mine. The charge for trespassin' on my property." She swung the boots around to irritate him. "Now go on, git!"

"I ain't leavin' without my boots!" Bill said.

"Your choice," she sighed, "but it's gettin' dark, ain't it?"

Bill looked around fearfully.

Josie cackled. "Doesn't that leader of yours say that evil comes out in the dark and—"

Bill backed away. "Rutherford says witches harvest their gardens by the light of the moon, when they turn natural things into evil things."

"I guess I should be gettin' back to my garden, now that you mentioned it." Josie cackled again.

Bill looked in her basket. "Those are evil things in there, aren't they?"

"These?" Josie said, sifting through the herbs in her basket. "Just a few things from Mother Nature's cupboard."

"Evil things . . . witch's things," Bill whispered.

"You leavin' or not?" Josie asked.

"I want my boots," Bill snapped.

Rubbing her back, Josie whispered, "Guess I'll just have to make you leave." Slowly, Josie turned around, winking at Laura.

"Hocus-pocus, web of fear,

Make this hunter disap—"

"Stop it, witch!" Bill screamed out.

Josie inched toward him, waving her cane in circles in the air. "You called me a witch again. You better be careful of what I can do."

Brother Bill backed into the bushes. "Jackson Rutherford ain't gonna like this. No sir. He ain't gonna like his dinner bein' taken, not one bit."

"Tell him to eat vegetables instead," Josie laughed.

"You'll have to answer to him," Brother Bill shouted over his shoulder.

"Not me. He didn't send me out to bring back dinner!" Josie laughed again, and spun around in circles, stomping her left foot on the ground. "Hocus-pocus, hunters and sinners, Bill's goin' home without the dinner."

Bill tripped over a log and Josie's laughter echoed off the hills. Laura couldn't help shivering, as the laughter lingered in the descending twilight.

Josie turned to Laura. Her broad smile made her warts jut out at odd angles. "Durn snake handlers. Wish they'd all go back to where they came from."

"What'd you want his boots for?" Laura asked.

Josie hung them over her shoulder and smiled. "Come on, follow me," she said, picking up her herb basket and setting off into the twilight.

CHAPTER 2

BLIND MAN'S HOLIDAY

Laura had only seen Josie a few times in her twelve years living in Mansfield. She was the old woman of the woods who rarely came to town.

Kids called her a witch and hunters were warned to keep off her property, though the boundaries of the land she claimed were never quite clear.

Local hunters complained that she'd spring from the bushes, almost out of nowhere, and scare off their game. Scared them too. Josie just wanted her animals left alone in the woods she roamed gathering herbs.

Laura and Manly had heard the tales about Josie, but when asked, Manly would say, "Don't ever see her and she don't borrow nothin'. Best neighbor we've ever had."

Now Laura followed behind the old woman, trying to figure her out. *She's a strange one,* Laura thought. *I want to like her but she's so . . . so different.*

Josie maintained a fast pace through the woods. Though Laura was at least thirty years younger, she had to step quickly to keep up. Josie followed an unmarked path like it was the main road through Mansfield. Each step was taking Laura farther away from Apple Hill Farm, down an unfamiliar darkened path.

"Carry my basket," Josie said, stopping to catch her breath. "I got my hands full."

Laura took the leaf-filled basket. "What's all this?"

Josie dug her cane in and started back on the path again. "Just some slippery elm bark and white oak bark."

Laura shrugged. "What do you use them for?"

"Me? I ain't blocked up, but got me an old geezer patient from up near Mountain Grove who ain't had a movement in two weeks."

"Patient? I didn't know you were a doctor."

Josie paused. "Way I was brought up, you didn't go to doctors. We fixed and dosed ourselves with the herbs all around us. Just self-reliant hill folks, we were."

Josie just kept walking and said over her shoulder, "Lots of folks have forgotten that there's medicine in the woods. People been callin' me an herb doctor so long that I got to callin' the folks that come see me patients."

Laura watched the old woman push through the underbrush. She had heard that the hill people came to Josie to be healed, but Laura now felt embarrassed. She'd just figured they were backward, superstitious folks who were afraid of doctors.

Pulling herself over a fallen tree, Josie said, "I ain't no book doctor, just learned about the woods from my grandma."

For a moment, Laura remembered Pa Ingalls, telling her about *the things that heal you in the woods—if you know what to look for.*

Josie stopped again. "Got me a lot of patients, I do. Old people with stomach pains, babies who need a little warm catnip tea to sooth away the fretfuls—all sorts of things."

Josie laughed and began walking. "When the leaves turn in the fall, why, I got me a whole troop of folks walkin' up here seekin' my cough medicine for croup. All I do is brew up honey, vinegar, and alum, and they think it's some kind of magical potion."

"Where are we going?" Laura asked, a bit worried.

Josie turned and laughed. "Laura Ingalls Wilder, you've been living in these parts for a long time, but you ain't never been to my cabin."

"I've never been invited," Laura said, catching her breath on the steep ridge.

"Well, you're invited now," Josie laughed, seeming to float up the ridge without effort.

All Laura could do was shake her head. *How can she be so strange and so likable at the same time?*

Josie pulled herself up over the boulder to the top and turned around to give Laura a hand. "Hurry, not too much farther."

Laura stopped to catch her breath. "Why the rush?"

" 'Cause it's a blind man's holiday," Josie said, as she started along the path again.

"A what?" Laura called after her, trying to follow the narrow path in the dark.

"It's a blind man's holiday, when twilight comes on," Josie said. She stopped and turned to Laura as she came to the far end of the ridge. "Look out here, Laura," she said, sweeping her arms in front of her as the sun set over the Ozarks. "It's too dark to read and not dark enough to light candles. That's why they call it a blind man's holiday. It's the time when the sighted eyes and the eyes of the blind come together as equals."

Laura had heard that Josie was a strange one and now considered it best to head back to Apple Hill Farm. Though not superstitious, walking through the dark woods with a cackling old woman gave Laura goose bumps. Old fears of what lay in the dark came back to her mind.

Right or wrong, it's human nature to be afraid of the unknown, Laura thought.

"Perhaps I could come visit you during the day. It's getting too dark for me to find my way home."

Josie laughed. "See this cane?" she asked, showing the carved face of an old man with closed eyes.

Laura looked at it and shuddered. "Yes . . . it's different."

Cackling with delight, Josie spun around. "It's my seeing-eye cane. Knows the woods better than I do. It gets me here and there, and it'll get you home. Don't you worry."

Josie took Laura by the arm and pointed with her cane down the ravine. "There's my cabin right down there."

Down below, hidden among the trees, was a split-timber cabin. Surrounded by odd-shaped gardens, planters, and cans and bottles filled with plants, it was every child's nightmare vision of the witch's house in the woods.

Laura had seen a witch's cabin like this in her childhood nightmares and felt her goose bumps rising. "My husband is expecting me and—"

Josie cackled. "Laura Ingalls Wilder! For a newspaper woman who pokes her nose into a lot of nobody's business, you're sure actin' nervous 'bout visitin' an old lady's cabin."

Laura sighed and nodded, shaking off a chill. "I guess I am. I've heard a lot about you and—"

Josie cut her off. "—and most of it whispered lies I'll bet."

Laura stammered. "I . . . I . . . don't know what . . ."

"You heard him call me a witch, didn't you?"

"Well, I . . ."

"Come on, tell me the truth. Just like you write in that column of yours," Josie said, with a mischievous sparkle in her eyes.

Laura liked the old woman's straightforward manner. "Yes, that's what some people say. But I don't believe it," Laura said, crossing her fingers. She quickly uncrossed them, feeling foolish for suddenly falling back on old superstitions.

Josie looked deep into Laura's eyes. "I think you're tellin' me the truth." She looked out over the Ozarks and screamed out, "She's tellin' the truth!" then shrieked with laughter.

The laughter echoed over the ridges and made Laura uncomfortable. More goose bumps rose on her arms.

Josie spun around and stamped her feet. "I'm just an ugly, old woman who gathers herbs. Don't be listenin' to that crazy bunch of snake handlers like that hunter."

"Snake handlers? Who are they?"

Josie shook her head. "Crazy man named Jackson Rutherford came up from Georgia. Brought him a pack of people that think he walks on water or somethin'. They pray to a big snake and think everyone but them is filled with evil."

"I've never met him . . . I've . . ."

Josie stopped Laura. "You will. I can sense it in my soul. But you be careful. The night wind that screams inside that man is darker than the blackest night."

"What kind of people pray to snakes?" Laura whispered, feeling the darkness wrap around her.

"Not snakes, I said snake. A big one. I think they call it Judgment." Josie shivered at the thought of the snake. "Every time I think of that monster snake, it gives me the willies."

"Is it some kind of pagan religion or something?"

Josie looked up at the sky, then directly at Laura. "Religion and me ain't got much in common. I ain't got nothin' against it, but don't have much use for those who use it for their own ends."

"What do you believe in?" Laura asked quietly.

Josie spun around again and tapped the ground with her cane, doing a one-legged jig. "I believe God made the earth and the goodness of nature. I believe that we are known by the way we live our lives."

Josie dropped to the ground and listened. "You got to have ears close to the ground to catch Mother Nature's clues. To find the answers to the mysteries of life."

Laura momentarily backed away, but Josie jumped up and grabbed her arm. "I ain't nothin' to be afraid of if you got common sense. There's always an ugly old crow in every town that becomes the bogie for the ignorant. But anyone who plays and prays with a snake is crazier than what folks think I am."

"You've seen them?" Laura asked.

Josie shook her head. "Just once, when they arrived. I've heard their talk and watched them in the woods. They call me a witch 'cause they can't find me when I follow 'em."

"Where do they live?" Laura asked.

"On the old abandoned Williams place. Live in the barn, they do. Put a down payment on it, then came and offered me money for my land. Sweet as punch, they were. Why, they even ate from my garden."

Laura didn't know what to say. For the second time that day, she was tongue-tied.

Josie snorted and stamped her foot. "But when I turned 'em down, that Jackson Rutherford told his people that I was the evil witch of the woods, that he had been brought to these parts to drive me away."

She spun around and looked at Laura. "My grandfather home-steaded this property. Got one hundred and sixty acres of nature's finest. I wouldn't sell it for a million dollars!"

"I love this land too," Laura whispered, finally able to speak.

Josie nodded. "Living here is where I'm happy. I don't need much and what I need the land gives me."

"Isn't it lonely, living by yourself?" Laura asked.

Josie smiled and pointed with her cane. "My ma and pa are buried over there, so I got them to talk to when I get the urge."

Laura didn't know if Josie was being serious and Josie laughed. "Laura Wilder, do I make you nervous? Tell the truth."

"I guess you kind of do," Laura shrugged.

"Well, don't let me get you worried. I haven't had someone to talk to for a bit, so I'm just playin' with you."

"But isn't it lonely out here living all alone?" Laura asked, warming up to the old woman.

"Just sort of seemed natural stayin' on after my folks died. I was never no beauty, so no menfolk came around. And without gettin' married, I never had no kids."

A bird flew up and tried to land on Josie's arm; then a deer appeared out of nowhere to nuzzle against her. "Go on, I don't have nothin' to feed you now," she laughed. She looked at Laura. "Guess the animals of the woods are my children."

The deer turned his head toward Laura, then melted back into the bushes. Josie cackled with laughter. "Just like the whitetail deers have nature's best eyesight and a sense of smell that can find an acorn in a storm, I know the woods."

"They shouldn't call you a witch," Laura said.

Josie sighed. "If the snake handlers can't see me watchin' 'em, it's not my fault. When it gets dark, I'm usually in plain sight, but they're scared of the dark."

"Why?"

Josie put her face up to Laura's. "They think that when darkness falls, that the evil ones come out—evil ones like me." She pulled on her largest chin wart and whispered, "I'm no witch, Laura Ingalls Wilder, I'm no witch."

Laura crossed her arms, trying to hold off a shiver. "I . . . I don't think you are."

"That means you believe in witches?" Josie asked.

"No . . . I didn't say that . . . it's just . . ."

Josie looked again in Laura's eyes. "I may be able to feel what people are thinkin' and I may look as old as dirt, but I have a love for life. I live to help people with things that come from the earth, like this bark and these herbs," she said, running her hands through the basket. "Do you understand?"

"I . . . I think so," Laura said, quite taken aback by the intensity of the woman's stare.

"Do you know about the gifts of nature? About the herbs that are given to those who know where to look for them? About what they can do for the body?"

Laura nodded. "I learned a bit about herbs back on the prairie. Dr. George told me—"

Josie cut her off. "Doctors make their money off of seein' sick people. I help people stay healthy."

"Dr. George is different."

"He's still a doctor," Josie said stubbornly.

"I'd like to come talk with you about this sometime," Laura said, lifting Josie's hand from her wrist.

"When?"

"When what?" Laura asked.

"When you comin' to talk?"

"I'll come back this week."

Josie handed Laura her cane. "Here. You'll need this."

Laura hesitantly accepted the carved cane. "It's nice, but I couldn't."

Josie laughed. "You'll need it to find your way home. It'll help you in ways you don't realize."

For a brief moment Laura thought, *The old woman might actually think the cane has magical powers.*

Josie caught her hesitation and laughed again. "Laura, this ain't no witch's cane or broomstick. It'll help you along the path; give you some courage if you begin to hesitate."

That's reasonable, Laura thought. "Thank you. I'll bring it back when I come to talk with you."

Josie cackled. "That's my way of knowin' you'll come back. Take this along with you also," Josie said, reaching behind a large rock. She pulled out a lantern. "Left this in case it got too dark even for me to get down the cliff to my cabin." She struck a wooden match and lit the lantern.

"That's what I really need," Laura laughed, then stopped. Josie had stooped down and was tying the hunters bootlaces together.

"What are you doing?" Laura asked.

"Watch!" Josie cackled. She stood up and swung the boots around her head.

Laura watched, fascinated with the strange old woman. *Why is she throwing away the boots?* she wondered.

Josie let loose of the boots, into the night, out over the cliff.

"What'd you do that for?" Laura asked.

"I need a new pair of shoes to add to my shoe tree," Josie answered, trying to keep sight of the boots in the air.

"Your what?" Laura asked, her eyes fixed on the rapidly falling boots.

"My shoe tree. Hope they land next to Rutherford's," she giggled, then clapped as the boots caught on the branch of a tree below.

Laura thought she heard someone cry out down below, but passed it off as just sounds of the night.

Josie peered over the edge. "Yup, I think they landed right next to the king of the Flock's shoes. They can keep each other company. Four lost shoe souls hangin' in my tree," she cackled.

Laura looked through the twilight and couldn't believe her eyes. There was a shoe tree down there! An old oak tree filled with shoes.

Shoes of all sizes and all colors. Boots, walking shoes, dancing shoes—it was something right out of a fairy tale! *I must be dreaming,* Laura laughed to herself.

There seemed to be three large objects hanging in the tree, but Laura couldn't make out what they were. "What's the shoe tree for?" Laura asked, shaking her head, trying not to giggle.

Josie spit. "I keep my shoe tree for two reasons. One, I don't like to charge folks more than eatin' money for the herbs I give 'em, so I ask them to leave me their shoes. Most folks who know me bring along an extra pair so they don't have to walk home in their stocking feet." Josie cackled and spun around again.

Laura asked, "What's the second reason?"

"Thought you'd never ask," Josie cackled. "My second reason for havin' the shoe tree is for those folks too poor to buy new shoes. I let 'em climb the tree and pick themselves a pair. It's my way of sharin' the road that we all walk on together."

Laura began smiling at the childish simplicity of it. "It makes sense."

"Of course it makes sense!" Josie snapped, clearly irritated. "You don't have to write for a newspaper to see that!"

Laura was caught off guard. "I was just saying—"

"Life makes sense if we eat what nature gives us and share what we have."

"Like sharing shoes," Laura smiled.

Josie, thinking that Laura was mocking her, said coldly, "Ain't nothin' wrong with walkin' in the other feller's shoes awhile. Humbles the mighty and lifts up the weak."

For the third time that day, Laura was speechless.

Josie spun around again, then looked up. "Star light, star bright, I just saw the first star tonight."

Laura looked at the twinkling star and tried to make conversation. "We're all alone in this universe. So we should try to get along together."

Josie pointed to the stars on the horizon. "Laura Ingalls Wilder, we're not alone! There's life out there," she said, raising her arms to the heavens.

"But where's the proof?" Laura asked, enjoying the agile mind of the old woman.

"Proof?" Josie shouted. "If you consider that there's only life on earth and nothing on those countless planets out there, why that's as silly as thinkin' that if you sow an entire grainfield, that only one plant will grow."

Laura stared at the stars that kept popping out in the darkening sky. "I've never thought of it that way."

"There's nothin' wrong with thinkin'," Josie said quietly. "It's only when you let others do the thinkin' for you that you end up like them folks from Georgia, prayin' to snakes and bein' slaves to that man."

"What was his name?"

"Rutherford. Jackson Rutherford. The snake handler who dresses in black."

CHAPTER 3

SHOE TREE

Larry, Terry, and Sherry Youngun, children of Mansfield's widowed Methodist minister, were hiding in the shoe tree down below. Sitting in their stocking feet, they'd been trying on shoes, hoping to find some that fit.

The shoe tree was a whispered legend around Mansfield, and the Younguns had decided to see if it was true. They couldn't believe it when they came upon the tree with hundreds of shoes, dangling from the branches.

Awoooooooooooo. Their dog Dangit was waiting at the base of the tree and had begun to whine.

Ten-year-old Larry Youngun, rubbed his head where the hunting boots Josie had thrown down had hit him. "Quiet, Dangit. She'll hear you." The dog stopped whining.

Larry looked up. "Hope she don't throw any more boots down. Those clompers almost killed me," he whispered.

Sherry, his five-year-old sister, stared toward the top of the ridge. "Wish she'd throw down some pretty red shoes. That's what I want."

Her seven-year-old brother, auburn-haired Terry, shook the branch. "If she throws any girlie shoes down, I'm jumpin'."

"Might hurt yourself," whispered Larry.

"Better than bein' hit by a witch's girlie shoes. Might turn me into a girl or somethin' terrible like that."

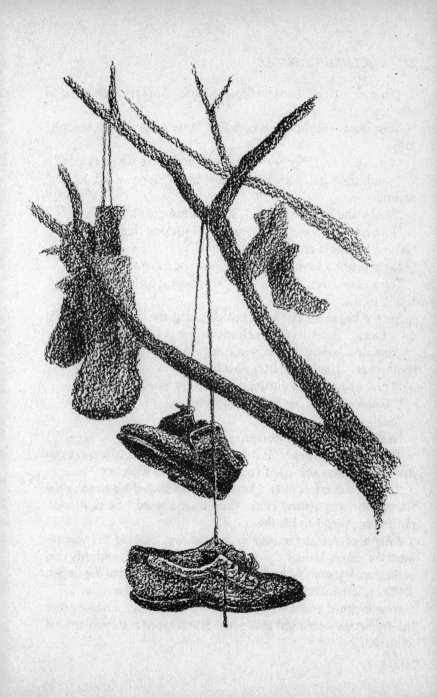

"That ain't true," Larry whispered back. "Ain't no such thing as witches."

"Just like there ain't no shoe trees," Terry snapped back sarcastically.

"Yes, there are," Sherry whispered, "and we're sittin' in one."

"Think she's got a toy tree around here?" Terry asked, looking around.

"Maybe she has a doll tree," Sherry whispered hopefully.

"I don't think so," Terry sneered, sticking his tongue out. "Who'd be stupid enough to plant one?"

Larry heard a sound. "Shhh. I think she's comin' back."

Terry leaned over to his sister. "Witches eat little girls," he said, trying to scare her.

Sherry began to cry and crawled along the branch, grabbing onto Larry. "Don't let her cook me in her pot."

"She ain't no witch," Larry said as he rubbed her head, trying to soothe her. "That's just talk. Now be quiet."

"Then why are you shushing up?" Terry asked smiling.

" 'Cause we're in her tree," Larry replied.

"So?"

"So be quiet!" Larry whispered harshly.

Terry shook his head. "If she ain't no witch, then why don't you just go on down and ask if you can eat supper with her?"

" 'Cause I don't want to," Larry said. He cocked his head to the sound. She was getting close. "Don't say a word," he cautioned, putting his finger to his lips.

Josie appeared at the edge of the clearing, making her way toward the cabin. Dangit crawled out from the bushes with his ears perked up, but crawled back in when he saw Larry's shaking finger.

"There's the witch," Terry whispered, his eyes wide.

Josie laughed as she walked beneath the shoe tree, unaware that the Younguns were right above her. She stopped and spun around in a circle.

"Think I'm a witch, do they?" she cackled. "Then where's my witch's broom?"

The Younguns shivered as her laughter echoed across the hollow. Dangit put his paws over his ears.

Terry whispered, "I bet her broom's on the porch. That's where witches keep their flyin' brooms."

"Who said that?" Josie screamed, looking around. "Who's trespassin' on my land?"

The Younguns paled, hoping that Josie's eyesight wasn't very good.

Josie sniffed the air. "Ah-hah! There's someone round here. I can smell you!"

The three Younguns looked at each other. Terry mouthed, "Not me" and Sherry mouthed, "I didn't do it." They didn't know that Josie had seen them from the corner of her eye.

Josie laughed loudly and sniffed the air again. "I can smell your feet." She sniffed again. "Six legs and thirty toes. All hooked to six little feet."

Terry began counting his toes, starting with the big toe which was sticking through a hole in his sock.

"Six feet," Josie giggled, "the measure of a coffin under the ground."

The Younguns' eyes were as wide as saucers. Sherry clung to Larry.

Josie spun in circles. "Come out, come out, wherever you are."

"I ain't goin' down," Terry whispered.

"Who said that?" Josie screamed.

Terry started to speak but Larry clamped his hand over his mouth.

Josie continued spinning, stomping her left foot on the ground. "Fe, fi, fo, fum, I smell some smelly children." She looked around and cackled, then continued. "Be they alive or be they dead, I'll grind their bones to make my bread."

"Oh Lord," Larry moaned, "we're in a beanstalk tree."

"Beanstalk!" Sherry moaned. "That's where the giant lives!"

Josie heard them and looked up. Children had been calling her a witch for so many years, that it had become second nature to play the game with them.

"You children come down here right now!"

"No!" screamed Terry.

"Come down here," Josie insisted.

"You're gonna grind our bones," Sherry whimpered.

"I was just thinkin' about it," Josie chuckled.

"You were thinkin' 'bout eatin' some bone bread!" Terry screamed. "We ain't gonna let no witch lock us up and cook us."

"It's gettin' dark," Josie cackled, spinning around. "Ain't you scared to be up there?"

"Better scared up here than gettin' eaten down there!" Larry said back.

Josie struck a match. The glow momentarily showed the three Younguns. "Ain't you the minister's kids?" she asked, peering through the fading match light.

They all nodded their heads, too scared to speak.

"I said, ain't you the minister's kids?"

"Yes, and we want to go home," Sherry whimpered.

"Well, come on down. I'll show you the way home," Josie said softly. "I ain't gonna hurt ya."

"I ain't comin' down until you leave," Terry said, shaking his head.

Josie smiled and lit another match. "Where do you want me to go? This is my land."

"Don't matter to me where you go," Terry snapped, glaring back. "Go haunt a house or somethin'!"

"We don't like witches!" Sherry whimpered through her tears.

Josie nodded. She was used to children calling her names. "And how do you want me to leave—walk?"

"Just get on your broom and fly away!" Sherry screamed.

"Make yourself disappear," Larry said, clearing his throat.

"Thought you didn't believe in witches!" Terry whispered to Larry.

Larry whispered back, "I'm sittin' in a shoe tree so I don't know what to believe."

Josie spun around again. "Alright, let me get on my broom and fly away."

She walked toward her rickety old cabin, making a lot of noise, enjoying the game. "Ah-hah! Here's my flyin' broom," Josie exclaimed, lighting a match.

The Younguns looked over and saw her holding an old broom. "She *is* a witch," Larry muttered.

"Any of you kids want to ride?" Josie asked, opening a jar. She began smearing a thick gel on her face.

"What's that stuff?" Terry asked.

"Flyin' ointment," Josie answered. "Need it to keep me up in the air." She put some on her crooked nose. "It ain't the broom that flies, that's just what I sit on."

The Younguns were all ears, sitting up in the tree. This was something they could brag about at school—if they lived to tell about it.

Josie giggled at the game she was playing. "Yup, I could fly on a cane or even a plow if I wanted."

"A plow?" Sherry whispered.

Josie wrapped her legs around the broom and smiled. "It's the ointment that makes you fly; this stuff right here," she said, holding the jar in front of them. "You want to put some on, little girl?"

"No!" Sherry screamed, hiding behind Larry.

Josie cackled. "Flyin' ointment's made from very potent herbs: monkshood, henbane, nightshake, hemlock, and blended with—"

She paused. The Younguns leaned forward and Josie winked at them. "—the fat of unbaptized children."

The Younguns gasped while Josie closed one eye to peer into the jar. She lit another match and looked in. "I've about run out. Say,"

she whispered, looking at the Younguns, "are you three kids bap-
tized?"

The Younguns were tongue-tied and just nodded.

"Rats!" Josie said, snapping her fingers. "Thought I could get
some fat off your pudgy bones. Oh well, time to fly away."

She waved to Terry. "Come on, Red, climb on and fly to the
moon with me."

"Forget it!" Terry shouted. "I wouldn't get on that thing for all
the candy in the world."

"Suit yourself," Josie laughed, picking up another jar with a red
lid. She began rubbing the new ointment on her face.

"What's that stuff?" Larry asked.

"Oh, just some disappearin' cream," Josie smiled, thinking
about the aloe vera and mint gel she was rubbing on her wind-
burned cheeks.

"What's it made of?" Terry asked.

"Ain't got time to talk," Josie said. "Got some flying to do." Josie
waved as the match faded. "See you kids later."

When the flame went out, she was engulfed in darkness. The
Younguns were unable to see that she had slipped off the edge of
the porch and was circling around the bushes toward the tree they
were in.

"She's gone!" Larry exclaimed.

"That disappearin' cream works fast!" Terry exclaimed.

"There she goes!" Sherry exclaimed, pointing up toward a shooting star.

"She's movin' fast!" Larry said, shaking his head in awe.

"Probably goin' to a bone bread party," Terry declared.

"Come on, let's get outta here," Larry nodded, "before she flies
back."

They scrambled down the tree, but Sherry saw a pair of red girl's
shoes and reached for them. "I want those shoes," she shouted.

"Leave 'em be," Larry said. "Pa wouldn't let you wear no fancy
shoes like that anyway."

Larry dropped to the ground. He reached back up and lifted Sherry down from the branch. Terry dropped from the other side.

"Get your shoes on, quick," Larry said.

Dangit crawled out and stood beside Larry, with his ears up for danger. "Let me know if you see her, boy," Larry said. "Come on, Terry, put your shoes back on."

Terry, dusted himself off and looked up. "Where'd she get all those shoes anyway?"

Josie popped out of the bushes. "By takin' the shoes from little trespassers like you!"

Dangit started barking and rushed toward Josie, who kicked the dog away. Sherry screamed and Larry fell over Terry.

Josie jumped forward and grabbed Sherry by the arms. "Got ya'!"

"Don't eat us!" Terry screamed.

"Dangit, I ain't gonna eat you!" Josie said, shaking them.

Uh-oh, Terry thought to himself, *she said the wrong thing.*

Dangit, who didn't like anyone to misuse his name, charged forward. Before Josie could kick him away, he'd grabbed hold of the hem of her long skirt and was ripping off the lining.

"Get this dog off me!" Josie screamed, trying to stomp on Dangit's feet. Sherry slipped free and ran behind Larry.

"Stop, Dangit, stop!" Larry shouted, and the dog backed off and hid behind him.

Josie was clearly irritated and looked them over. "Now I'm gonna teach you all a lesson."

"For what?" said Larry, eyeing her carefully, wondering if he was going to have to fight his way out.

"For you trespassin' and lettin' that dog rip my skirt."

"What you gonna do?" Terry asked.

"I said I'm gonna teach you a lesson. I want your dog."

"For what?" Terry asked.

"I need me a good watchdog. But if he bites me again, I'll just have to eat him," she cackled, enjoying the game.

"Can't have him," Larry said.

"Then," Josie sighed, pointing to their feet, "I guess it's your shoes."

"Shoes? What about 'em?" Terry demanded.

"I want 'em!" Josie said.

"I don't got no other shoes," Sherry whimpered.

"They won't fit you!" Larry huffed.

"I got stinky feet. You don't want smelly shoes, do you?" Terry said.

"They'll air out overnight."

"But I got holes in my socks," Terry sniffed.

"Take off your shoes," Josie snapped, pointing her cane at them, "and tie the laces together."

"But these are our school shoes!" Larry protested.

Josie laughed. "So? There's lots of poor kids who need shoes."

"But we need our shoes," Sherry moaned.

"Then I guess it's dinner then," Josie said. "You either come eat dinner with me or give me your shoes for trespassin' on my property."

Terry sat right down and began unlacing his shoes. "You can have mine! I ain't goin' in no witch's house. No sir, I'd rather starve than eat bone bread."

"That's a good boy," she said patting his head.

"Keep your hands off my hair," Terry snapped.

"Such pretty auburn hair. Mind if I keep some?" she asked, pulling several long hairs out.

"Ouch!" Terry screamed.

"Where did you get your pretty auburn hair?" she asked, looking at the long strands.

"It came with my head," Terry glared, rubbing where it hurt.

"You'll be all right," she laughed. "Now give me your shoes before I take some more of your hair."

"Now can I leave?" Terry asked, handing her his shoes.

"Yes," Josie answered, "and don't come back without bein' asked."

"Have a nice bone bread dinner," Terry said, slapping Larry on the back. He started walked away.

"Where you goin'?" Larry shouted out.

Terry stopped and turned. "I'm goin' home to move your stuff out of my room. Ain't no reason to be sharin' a room with a dead-duck brother."

Sherry kicked off her shoes and hurried behind Terry. Larry looked at Josie who was cackling to herself. "You like scarin' little kids?"

"Just give me your shoes."

Larry untied his laces and handed the shoes to her. "You ain't no witch, but you sure are strange."

Josie patted him on the head. "No stranger than you sneakin' on my property and sittin' in my shoe tree," Josie said, taking Larry's shoes.

"What are we goin' to tell our Pa?" Larry asked.

Josie laughed. "Your Good Book says to tell the truth," she said. "Start with that."

"Sometimes the truth hurts," Terry called out. "Pa's gonna whup us fur sure."

Josie shrugged. "Just tell him you gave your shoes to help the poor. That's close to the truth like horseshoes."

"But—," Larry protested.

Terry ran up and grabbed him by the arm. "But nothin'! That's the kind of truth-tellin' that will keep our behinds from gettin' strapped. Come on, we gotta go!"

As the Younguns ran off through the dark hills, Josie's cackling laughter echoed around them. Dangit howled back in defiance—from a safe distance.

"Those kids will believe anything," Josie laughed to herself.

She tied the laces of the shoe pairs together and flung them up into her tree. Then she stuck the strand of Terry's hair into her pocket and picked up her herb basket.

She didn't know that Terry had doubled back around to watch, sneaking by her to get to the porch. He saw the jars of flying cream and disappearing cream and thought about taking them, but was scared.

Then he saw her broom and reached over to feel the straw, plucking some off. Next to it was a brush with long gray hairs stuck in the bristles.

"Fair is fair," Terry whispered, pulling out some of her hair.

CHAPTER 4

SNAKE HANDLERS

Bill Ponder, Brother Bill, walked through the twilight with his head hung low. It had been his assignment to shoot a deer. It had been part of the vision. The Flock was depending on him.

Now he was coming back empty-handed.

With his wife and three children, Bill had followed Jackson Rutherford to the Ozarks. The trip from Jonesboro, Georgia, had taken ten weeks, but Rutherford kept them going with visions of the promised land. Ten families had come on the walk, all members of his Flock of Life with Signs Leading, as Rutherford had named it.

They had all come together two years before, seeking new meaning from Scripture. At first, Bill accepted Rutherford's revelation that the only word they needed was his. "I have seen the writing in the sky. The way has been pointed," he'd tell the Flock. But things began to change long before they moved West.

Rutherford's visions became more bizarre. He saw evil beings that he claimed only he could see. He had visions of who were traitors and who could be trusted. And when he had the vision that the big snake could point the way, Bill began worrying for his family.

He wasn't alone. Others in the Flock were grumbling. Rutherford noticed it too and put the blame on the evil influences of nearby Atlanta.

"I will go off alone into the wilderness and find the answer,"

Rutherford told them, mixing Scripture with his own blend of opportunism.

So he went into the woods to pray and came back with the vision of the promised land. Though the vision was probably aided by an article he'd read about the Ozarks in an old newspaper he found on his walk, it was a way to keep his Flock together.

Having followers was part of his visions, and being away from the corruption of the rest of the world was his foundation. Once in Mansfield, Rutherford left his Flock in the woods and went into town alone. *Only he* was strong enough to ward off evil influences.

He put a down payment on the abandoned Williams farm and moved the Flock into the barn, the only structure still standing. They lived a communal life that Rutherford said was the way, sharing food and doing the work assigned them.

Rutherford lorded over his Flock, cutting an imposing figure. He dressed in black, carried a staff, and with a voice louder than a mountain storm, controlled the Flock through fear and intimidation.

His word was the way. He changed Scriptures to fit his needs. He played on superstitions and his own visions to set the rules that the Flock lived by. No discussion or dissent was tolerated.

Rutherford saw evil everywhere: in everything, in everybody. His visions told him that he had been put on earth to root out evil and to save mankind. When twilight came, he would huddle the Flock together to warn them about the legions of the night. With nothing more than candles to keep out the dark world, his paranoia about evil became uncontrollable.

Long used to getting his way, Rutherford wanted more property. He needed it to fulfill his vision of leading an isolated tribe in a simple life away from the evils of civilization.

From the ridges he spied Apple Hill Farm, but it looked too prosperous. With its well-tended orchards, fields, and cattle, Rutherford put obtaining Apple Hill Farm on a list of things that would happen later.

But on the other side, he saw the untouched lands of Josie Tatum. He knew from asking around town that she was a recluse. Some said she was senile.

So he went to Josie, intent upon persuading her to sell or give him her land and join his Flock. At first he tried Scripture and brought her gifts. He admired her herb garden and exchanged cures that he'd been taught by his own grandma in Georgia. He went so far as to freely give his shoes for her shoe tree.

Josie saw him coming from a distance and played along. She was used to the sharpies and the fast talkers who assumed that just because she lived by herself in the hills, she was ignorant. And Rutherford wasn't the first one who'd tried to buy her out or steal her land.

But Josie saw something different about Rutherford. She knew his gifts and front porch talk were all part of some kind of act. Behind the dark eyes was a bad and troubled man.

When Josie wouldn't sell him her adjoining land, Rutherford had found his first sign of evil in the woods. Driving Josie out had become a personal obsession of his. She became his scapegoat.

For the first several weeks, he went at twilight to the ridge above her house and shouted, "Out, witch, out!" But Josie just ignored him, thinking he'd soon tire of the game.

But it wasn't a game to Rutherford. Night after night, he ranted on. "The witch's garden is filled with the red berries of yew, monkshood, nightshade, and other plants. Some are the color of corpses." Walking with a candle in his hand, he'd whisper, "She fertilizes her plants with dead souls and makes her witch's concoctions from demon animals." Sometimes Josie would sneak over to the farm and listen to his rantings.

Tonight, the only thing on Brother Bill's mind was failure—his failure to fulfill Rutherford's vision and bring back a deer. As he approached the ramshackle old barn, he could hear Rutherford's booming voice preaching to the Flock.

"My visions are the way. They show the signs."

Bill did not want to go in. He had failed in his task. He knew what the punishment would be for coming back empty-handed.

Inside, Rutherford waved his arms in the twinkling candlelight. His Flock of thirty-five men, women, and children sat on the old hay they'd spread on the floor. They watched in fear and fascination as the man in black railed about the evil around them.

"Each of you has grown weak. You are lacking in spirit."

The Flock mumbled in unison, "Yes. Yes. Yes."

Rutherford clapped his hands for silence. "I feel evil creeping into the room. I want to grab it by the throat and shake the life from it."

He opened the slats of the window, then slammed it shut. "Somewhere, just right out there, is a patchwork quilt of an animal. I can sense it. It's got cat's claws, goat's hoofs, and a human face so wretched that to look at it can stop your heart."

Fear swept through the Flock.

"That's right. Huddled just out there, beyond the trees, is evil, waiting to corrupt those who stray from the true path of the signs leading."

He stopped in front of a group of Flock children, who cowered back from him. "Are you evil?" he asked them loudly. The wide-eyed children shook their heads no.

Rutherford turned to three women sitting on a hay bale. "Do you feel choked by your false pride, your craving for worldly goods, your dark desire, born from evil's sorcery?"

"No, no," one of the women mumbled.

"I think you need to be cleansed," Rutherford said. "One of you needs to be cleansed. Which one shall it be?"

Rutherford looked back and forth between them. The women dropped their heads, not wanting to be chosen.

Bill tried to slip in unannounced, but the sound of the creaking door alerted Rutherford. "How big a buck did you bring us?"

Bill looked down and said, "He was eight points."

Rutherford walked toward him, leaving the relieved women behind. "Eight points! We will feast for days on fresh venison!"

He walked around the room, beaming. "Didn't I tell you I had a vision? Brother Bill has brought it back for us!"

For the first time since entering the barn, the people in the room were smiling. Fresh meat was a luxury, since there never seemed to be enough to go around. After Rutherford ate what he called "the first rightly share," it was then left for the men to eat, then the women, and finally the children, who always looked hungry.

Rutherford's rules were simple and direct. He owned everything. They owned nothing. All food was his to eat and his to give. Those caught breaking the rules had to be cleansed.

Rutherford pushed open the barn door, looking for the eight-point buck. "Well, where is it?"

"The old witch woman scared the buck away," Bill said, looking down.

"She what?" Rutherford screamed.

"As I pulled the trigger, she hit me with a rock and my shot went wide."

"Where were you?" Rutherford said coldly, his face red with anger.

"I was sitting in the crook of the tree, rubbing the antlers together like you taught me."

"And you say the old woman threw a rock up into the tree?" Rutherford's face showed disbelief. "She's too old to toss one above her head."

Brother Bill raised his head and looked into Rutherford's eyes. "Then she used her witchcraft to knock my rifle away."

"Where are your boots?" Rutherford screamed.

"She took them," Brother Bill whispered.

Rutherford looked outside into the darkness. "Out in the night, the powers of darkness are trying to work their evil. Rocks flying. Witches laughing. It's all out there," he pointed.

Closing the barn door and sliding the bolt, he turned. "That witch is probably doing the devil's dance in your boots." He began dancing around with a maniacal grin on his face. "Oh yes, she's dancin' in your boots, holdin' on to your soul."

Then he abruptly stopped and covered his face. The whole room went silent. "You aren't tellin' me everything." He looked up and asked, "Did you eat from her garden? Did she offer you any witch's tea? Did she try to make you dance in the moonlight?"

"No . . . no," Bill stammered. "I kept my distance."

"Did she say she had fresh-cut sassafras root, boiling just inside?" Rutherford asked, moving forward. "Did she try to lure you to sin?"

Bill shook his head. "No . . . I resisted it all."

He put his arm around Brother Bill. "You have been around a witch. Your soul has been touched by evil. You need to be cleansed."

"No, please, no," Brother Bill pleaded. "I was cleansed last week. It is not my time. You said I wouldn't need it again until the harvest."

Tightening his grip on Bill's shoulder, Rutherford nodded to a burly man standing in the back shadows of the barn. "Brother Robert, bring out the crate. We need to search his soul for the true signs of life leading."

"It is not right," Brother Bill's wife Susan called out.

"Woman, you be quiet or you'll be next!" Rutherford commanded.

Susan Ponder sat back down, tears in her eyes, holding her two huddled children in her arms. Three-year-old Carrie Ponder whimpered, but seven-year-old Tyler glared at Rutherford.

Bill tried to reassure her with his eyes, but failed because *he* was scared. "Leave my pa alone," young Tyler said.

Rutherford hit him with his staff. "You should be whipped for such insolence." He turned to his father. "Brother Bill, step forward. You have been chosen for cleansing."

Relieved that they were not being called on to be cleansed, the Flock edged forward. They were tense with excitement, attracted and repelled by their morbid fascination with what was to come.

As the crate was set down in front of the Flock, Rutherford stepped forward and hit his staff against the side. The rattle of the deadly snake's tail answered back.

Rutherford smiled. "The rattlesnake of the Flock is ready to test you for signs." He rapped the crate again. "The rattle of this snake separates it from all other snakes in the world. That's why he's special."

The sound of the rattlesnake's tail subsided, so Rutherford hit against the crate for a third time. The snake responded.

"That's better. Just like a baby will cry after being brought into this world, a baby rattler's tail will vibrate moments after birth. And just like a human, the rattle gets louder as it grows larger, shedding its skin."

He paused and smiled to Bill. "Are you ready?" Bill looked down, trying not to tremble.

Rutherford reached in and petted the thick diamondback rattler. The rough-scaled, thick-bodied snake licked out its tongue.

"This snake's got a hair-trigger temperament," Rutherford said, stroking the snake. "It can't stand evil."

The snake popped its head out of the crate and the children cowered against the wall. Rutherford stroked the back of the snake's head and smiled. "Rattlers are like humans. They give birth to live young, just like you came out of your mothers." The children backed away as the snake inched out a foot, then pulled its head back in.

"There are all kinds of rattlesnakes," he said. "Prairie rattlers, sidewinders, black-tailed rattlers, swamp rattlers, and other snakes which can kill. But no one has what we've got." He paused, reaching back into the crate. "Yes, sir, we've got the king of snakes," he said, pulling out the eight-foot, twenty-pound eastern diamondback.

The children covered their eyes and the men gasped. No one, not even the believers, liked to be near this snake. This was the one that had found evil in six of their Flock they'd left in Georgia—in unmarked graves.

"This is Judgment, the snake that finds signs of true evil." Rutherford played with the big, dark, dangerous snake, then lifted it over his head, letting it coil up in front of him. "This is the most dangerous snake in the world, but you got nothin' to fear if you're free of evil."

Walking around the room, he asked his Flock, "Do you think that the signs of life leading are here to be read?"

The Flock mumbled agreement. He held the awesome thing in front of Brother Robert, the true loyalist among his followers. Robert didn't flinch as the snake darted back and forth around his face.

"You see," Rutherford smiled, "Brother Robert is free of evil."

Rutherford turned as the monster snake spun its head around, striking out but missing his own face. Rutherford laughed. "This snake is looking for signs. Does he find them among you?" he asked, walking among the Flock.

The snaked slithered its tongue in and out, ready and waiting. In the middle of the barn, Rutherford spun around. "Brother Bill. Catch!" he shouted, tossing the rattlesnake into the air.

Susan Ponder screamed, trying to shield her children's eyes, but Tyler wiggled free. "Don't, Pa, don't!"

Bill caught the snake in midair and went to drop it back in the crate. Judgment coiled, not wanting to go in. It was a cat-and-mouse game with the snake, but Bill was the mouse.

Then the huge snake's rattler began again. It sounded like a drum beating, like a thousand tongues fluttering.

Bill's wife gasped as the snake opened its mouth. The fangs were erect, ready to bite.

It struck out at Bill, missed, and recoiled to strike again. Then, it was all over. Judgment retracted his fangs, closed his mouth, hanging limp in Bill's hand.

Rutherford smiled. "Judgment is known to only strike out once like that." But the snake's rattle started again, silencing the room.

Rutherford's eyes widened. "Has Judgment found a sign? Perhaps a hidden sign that we cannot see?"

A film of sweat broke on Bill's forehead. He was trying to stay calm, but Judgment's head was wiggling back and forth in front of his face. Then the snake hung limp again.

Bill quickly tried to put the snake back into the crate. As he closed the lid, he turned to Rutherford. "I am free. I am free of evil and—"

Before he could complete his sentence, he spun around in agony. The fangs of the gigantic Georgia rattler were sunk deeply into his wrist!

Susan screamed and his children cried out. "No, Pa, no!" Tyler screamed.

Bill tried to shake the snake loose, but its fangs were in too deep. The poison was rushing through his veins.

It was a dance with death. Bill knew he was going to die. It was the life or death element that all knew existed in Jackson Rutherford's cleansing ceremony.

Bill's eyes went white and he collapsed into a twitching heap of agony on the floor. Susan rushed to her husband's side.

"Get her away!" Rutherford shouted.

"Save the children," Bill whispered to his wife, before two men in the Flock pulled her back at Rutherford's command.

When the last spasm stopped, Rutherford stepped forward and pulled the snake loose. With blood dripping from its fangs, Rutherford put Judgment back into the crate and snapped the lid shut.

He turned to his Flock. "There was evil among us and now—it is gone."

Without being asked, Brother Robert lifted up the body and took it out into the dark.

"Leave him nearby, so the evil ones can see how we deal with them," Rutherford said. "We'll bury him tomorrow when the noon sun gives the sign."

Susan Ponder put her hands over her eyes and wailed as her husband's body was taken from the barn.

CHAPTER 5

SUMMERS ON THE LINE

Without Josie's lantern, Laura would have had a hard time finding her way back to Apple Hill Farm. The full moon was playing hide and seek with the clouds, and she was unsure of the path.

The gnarled old cane that Josie had lent her felt good in her hands. It was a protection against what lay beyond the lantern's light. Laura used it to push the bushes, test for loose rocks, and support herself up and down the ridges.

Stopping to catch her breath, she looked out across the ravine to her beloved farm. The full moon slipped out from behind the clouds and Laura could see the apple trees snuggled against the hills.

The lights from her home glowed against the night. *Manly is probably worried,* she thought, *wondering where I am.*

She was right. Manly was worried. He had come in from checking the orchards, expecting to find Laura waiting for him. Instead, he found himself waiting in the darkness.

Thinking she was still up on the ridge, Manly had walked up to her thinking rock, checked by the pond and even back through the orchards, in case she'd gone for a walk. But she was nowhere to be found.

Finally, he just stared through the front windows, debating

whether to call their neighbor Maurice Springer to come help him search. Then he heard her approach and walked out onto the porch.

"Is that you, Laura?"

"It's me," Laura sighed, "and I'm bone tired."

"Where you been?" he asked, walking down the stairs to greet her. "I looked up at your thinking rock, but couldn't find you." He didn't want to let on how worried he'd been.

Laura pecked his cheek and handed him the lantern. "I went to follow a buck and ran into Josie."

"Josie? You were out walkin' in the dark with a witch," he laughed, smiling mischievously.

Laura shook her head. "She may be strange, but she's no witch. You know, I kind of liked her."

"What's that in your hand?" he asked, reaching for the gnarled cane.

"Oh this? Josie gave it to me to guide me home."

Manly looked at the closed eyes of the carved face and smiled. "You sure she didn't put a spell on you or somethin'?"

"How'd you know?" Laura asked, then grabbed her forehead.

Manly played along. "What kind of spell she put on you? One to make you easier to live with?"

Laura opened one eye and frowned. "No, she put a spell on me that—will let me beat you to the house!" she screamed, racing off.

Manly, who limped from a stroke back in the Dakotas, kicked the ground. "You tricked me again, woman!" He followed behind, carrying the lantern and cane.

During supper, they discussed their annual Apple Hill Farm get-together that was coming up on Saturday and the Founder's Day foot race on the 14th.

Manly shook his head. "Ten bucks is a big prize just for kids to race through the hills. Why, when I was little, we'd have raced two miles for a nickel."

"Times have changed, Manly," Laura nodded, "but the Bentleys are putting up the prize money again this year so it's not costing the town anything."

Later that evening, after she had told Manly all about her encounter with Josie and the shoe tree, Laura sat on the porch rocker lost in thought. Manly came out and sat beside her. "What you thinkin' 'bout?"

"About the prairie days—coming to Missouri, and Rose."

Manly nodded. "I wish Rose went to school 'round here."

Laura sighed. "We've talked about that, but the high school in New Orleans is the best thing we can do for her. It'll change her life."

"Changin' my life too," Manly lamented. "Sometimes my heart hurts 'cause I miss her so much."

"Girls don't get much chance in this country without an education."

Manly, sensing a political argument coming on, tried to change the subject. "Let's talk about somethin' else. What other things were you thinkin' about?"

Laura shrugged, smiling at the way he'd deftly maneuvered her away from discussing women not having the right to vote. She looked back over their farm and sighed. "Oh, I was just remembering how we came to find this place, and how it's changed."

"You remember leavin' the Dakotas in that old wagon, and landing here with barely nothin'?"

Laura nodded and thought back. They'd come to Missouri to start again—to find their promised land and make a last stand of salvaging their lives. It seemed like yesterday, not twelve years ago, when Manly had brought their wagon to a halt at the edge of this rugged farmland.

We were just a couple of tenderfoots, Laura thought smiling, *but we pulled it off.*

The ringing of the telephone disturbed their tranquility. Manly went inside to answer it, then came back out. "It's Summers. Somethin' 'bout meetin' you in the morning at Mom's Cafe."

"Did you hang up on him?"

"Naw, but he'd talk to a fence post just to shoot his mouth off. I just left him talkin' so I could come out and get you."

"Oh, Manly, that was rude!" she exclaimed, walking by him to get the kitchen phone.

Manly shrugged. When she was out of ear shot, he mumbled, "Better rude than to have that man give me cauliflower ear from listenin' too much."

Laura picked up the receiver hanging from the crank wall phone. Andrew Jackson Summers was still talking away. ". . . and Manly, did I ever tell you about the time back in '92 when I was coverin' that political convention and caught a couple of no-goods tryin' to rob the future president and—"

"Hello, Andrew, this is Laura. Whatever are you talking about?"

"Laura? I thought I was talkin' to Manly! What happened?" Summers asked.

"You like talking to yourself, Andrew?"

Summers sputtered on the phone. "You tell Manly that he shouldn't just go puttin' the phone down when I'm talkin'!"

"Calm down, Andrew, or *I'll* be putting the phone down."

Summers sighed. "I'm sorry. Just sometimes I get rolling on a good story and don't like to stop till it's over."

"Yes, Andrew, I know that from experience. Whatever do you want at this time of the night?"

"Laura, can you meet me for breakfast tomorrow morning at Mom's Cafe? I got someone you ought to meet and write about."

"Who?"

"That new rabbi, Max Stern. He's come all the way from Russia with this huge yiddle printing machine."

"A what?" Laura asked.

"A yiddle machine. Said he bought it in Brooklyn, New York, and brought it out here to print up a newspaper for the Jews of the prairie."

"A yiddle machine? What in heaven's name is that?"

"How do I know what a yiddle is? I've only met a couple of Jews in my life."

Laura thought for a moment. "Did he say yiddle or Yiddish?"

"Come to think of it, I think he said Yiddish," Summers chuckled. "What's that anyway?"

"Andrew, for a newspaperman, you sure aren't very worldly," Laura laughed. "Yiddish is the mother tongue of millions of Jews in Eastern Europe."

"Well, he showed me some printed lines from the yiddle machine and—"

Laura interrupted him. "Yiddish, not yiddle."

"Yiddle, piddle, whatever. Anyway, the rabbi showed me what the machine prints out. Strangest looking letters I've ever seen in my life." He paused. "You know, those yiddleish letters looked sort of like Chan's Chinese writin' to me."

"Yiddish, Andrew, Yiddish," she sighed, rolling her eyes. "What time do you want me to meet you at Mom's?"

"I told the rabbi to be there 'round seven thirty. Is that too early?"

"I'll be there," Laura said, scribbling a note on the pad in her purse.

"Okay, Laura, see you then."

"Thanks for calling, Andrew."

Before Laura hung up, Summers shouted out, "Laura, Laura."

"Yes, Andrew?" she said, putting the receiver back to her ear.

"Don't forget to ask him questions about this machine. I think it'd make a great story."

Laura walked back out to the porch. "Goodnight, Manly. I'm feeling kind of tired."

"What'd Summers want to talk about so gosh-durn bad?"

"He just wanted to tell me about a yiddle machine," she answered grinning, closing the screen door.

"A fiddle what?" Manly called after her as she walked away.

Laura sighed as she walked upstairs. From Josie to Brother Bill and then Summers and his yiddle machine, it had been a long day.

CHAPTER 6

MUD SHOES

Rev. Youngun sat in his study, trying to work on his upcoming sermon. With all the children in town thinking of nothing but the ten-dollar prize in the Founder's Day foot race, he thought he might speak about the sin of greed.

Try as he might, he couldn't get the words to come. All he could think about was the widow Carla Pobst in Cape Girardeau, Missouri: the only woman besides his late wife he'd ever kissed. For almost a year he'd been thinking about her. When the fever took Norma, he thought his heart had turned to stone. With three kids to raise and a church to run, his hands were full.

Then he'd seen Carla when she visited his church. Something had gone off in his heart like an explosion. Though he was shy around women, he found the nerve to take her buggy riding. He visited with her at a church social and then went by train to see her in Cape Girardeau.

Now she was coming back to Mansfield to see him and wanted to come to dinner at his house. To meet his children. To test the waters.

Rev. Youngun sighed and thought, *It'll either be the start of something great, or she'll never come back again.*

He hadn't told the kids yet and didn't know how to tell them. All he knew was that he had to tell them soon. Carla would be here in two days and was going with them to the party at Apple Hill Farm.

He heard something outside and looked up. *It must be the children, late again for dinner. If I don't teach them to come home on time, no telling what bad ways they'll fall into one day.*

Outside, the three Younguns approached the house cautiously. Larry just knew they were going to get caught. They'd lost their new shoes and let Terry talk them into another one of his schemes.

"You think Pa will notice?" Larry asked, looking down at his mud-covered feet.

"Mud don't look like shoes," Sherry protested.

"Brown feet are better than pink feet," Terry shrugged. "If we can sneak by Pa, he might just think we got our brown shoes on."

Sherry didn't like the feel of the mud squishing between her toes. "Why can't we just tell him the truth?"

Terry gave her a bop on the head. "You want to tell him that we trespassed in a witch's yard, and she took our shoes and threw them in a shoe tree?"

"He's gonna find out sooner or later," Larry sighed.

Sherry bopped Terry back. "And sooner is tomorrow morning when we don't got our school shoes on."

"No," Terry said, "that's later. It gives me more time to think of somethin'."

"Maybe we could wear our old shoes," Larry said.

"You think your big feet can still fit into those secondhand dancin' shoes?" Terry laughed. "You want to keep wearin' donated shoes?"

"Better than goin' barefoot," Larry fired back.

"I'd rather go barefoot than put on those clod-clompers again," Terry said, shaking his head. "If we can just sneak past Pa, we'll think of somethin' by morning."

"Shhh," Larry whispered, pointing to the porch, "he'll hear you."

He *had* heard. Rev. Youngun was standing on the porch with his arms crossed. "Where have you been?"

Dangit ran off toward the barn to hide.

"We were out exploring," Larry answered.

"Yeah," added Sherry, "we were looking at trees."

"Say your prayers!" screetched Beezer, the talking parrot, from inside the house.

"Be quiet, Beezer," Rev. Youngun snapped.

"You're pathetic," Beezer squawked quietly.

The children tried not to giggle.

"Well," their father said, "you better get on in and clean up. It's bedtime."

"What about dinner?" Terry asked.

"It was ready when you were supposed to be home. I put everything away. You can think about why you missed dinner until breakfast tomorrow morning."

Terry looked down at their mud-caked feet, wondering how they'd explain losing their shoes to Pa. "You go on in, Pa. I think we need to stay out here and think about missin' dinner."

"Let's go in," Sherry exclaimed. "I want to wash my—" Larry nudged her. Sherry mouthed "oops" and said, ". . . ah, er . . . wash my hands."

Rev. Youngun crossed his arms. "Come on in now. March." None of them moved. "I said, come on in."

Larry knew the jig was up and hesitantly marched up the stairs. Sherry followed behind. Terry waited in the dark shadows, trying to come up with a plan.

It came to Terry. "Pa," he said, pointing up. "Those stars sure are pretty, aren't they?"

Rev. Youngun looked up at the stars, not down at the muddy feet that were marching by him. "Go on up to your rooms and get ready for bed," he said, squinting. "Ah . . . there's the Big Dipper."

It looked like they were going to get away with it! Terry scooted up the stairs and fell into line behind Sherry. Rev. Youngun turned around to lower the porch light.

Beezer the parrot squawked. "Pathetic. Say your prayers."

"Wish Beezer would shut up," Terry whispered.

Rev. Youngun loosened his tie so he could look up easier. "And there's the Little Dipper." He removed the stick pin, but dropped it. "Daggone it," he said, reaching down to pick it up.

Then he saw them. The muddy tracks leading into the house. He traced them to the muddy feet.

"Halt! Stop right there!" he shouted after the children who were at the top of the stairs.

"Uh-oh," Terry whispered, "we're sunk."

"Look at this mud!" Rev. Youngun shouted. "Why didn't you clean off your shoes before you entered the house?"

Larry shrugged. "Sorry, Pa. We'll clean it up."

"You bet you will! Now get back on the porch and take those shoes off."

The three Younguns looked at each other. Terry grabbed hold of the situation and said, "OK, Pa, we'll get this mud right off our shoes."

"Mud's on my feet," Sherry whispered to Larry.

"I'll explain it to you later," Larry whispered back.

Larry and Sherry marched behind Terry through the screen door. Terry couldn't leave well enough alone and said, " 'Course, cleanin' off our shoes might get them wet, so we might have to go barefoot to school tomorrow and—"

Rev. Youngun shook his head. "Just be careful cleaning them, otherwise, you'll have to wear your old shoes to school tomorrow."

As their father closed the door to go back to the sermon he was working on in the study, Larry frowned. "Now what are we going to do?"

Terry winked. "We're going to wear our old shoes tomorrow and then—" He stopped, looking off into the twilight.

Sherry prodded him. "And then what?"

Terry turned with a tight grin on his face. "Then we're goin' back tomorrow and get our shoes from that old witch."

Rev. Youngun called out from the house. "Oh, children, I forgot to tell you that Carla Pobst is coming for a visit in two days and will be at our house for dinner."

Larry looked at Terry who looked at Sherry.

"What she comin' back for? More monkey business?" Terry asked his brother and sister.

"Maybe she's hungry," said Sherry.

Larry frowned. "I think she's comin' 'round to see if she wants to be our ma."

"Maybe she'll see somethin' she'll never forget," Terry grinned. "Come on, let's get cleaned up. I'm tired."

CHAPTER 7

SNAKE BIT

Sheriff Sven Peterson, the strapping Swede, looked at the bloated body. The dead man was middle-aged, about five ten, with a thick red moustache. Maurice Springer had found him while he was delivering a load of feed.

"Is this the way you found him, Maurice?" the sheriff asked.

"Yes, sir. Right under the lightning tree."

Peterson looked up at the landmark tree at the entrance to the old Williams place. With a body in front of it, it now had an eery feel to it.

Maurice shivered. "I just saw him and raced my wagon to find you."

Peterson turned the man over on his side and noticed the swollen arm. "Did you touch him or move anything?"

Maurice took off his hat and wiped his brow. "Touch him? You think I want to go 'round touchin' a dead body?"

"The dead ain't gonna hurt you none," Peterson said, touching the dead man's arm.

"Maybe yes, maybe no," Maurice said, looking away from the body. "My daddy taught me that dead bodies can give you diseases and other things."

The sheriff's mind was on the body. "What other things?" he asked, absentmindedly.

Maurice looked down at the dead man's face, and closed his eyes. He didn't want to see those vacant eyes looking back up at him.

"What other things?" Peterson asked again, looking up. "Open your eyes."

"Close his first," Maurice said, pointing down.

Sheriff Peterson shrugged and closed the dead man's eyes with his fingers. "Now, what other things?"

Maurice peeked through one eye, then seeing the closed eyelids below him, opened his. "Things like ghost sickness."

"Ghost sickness? What kind of hogwash is that?"

"You knows it's hogwash, and I knows it's hogwash. But it ain't every day that you come across a dead body."

"Thank God for that," Peterson said, lifting up the dead man's wrist.

"Amen," said Maurice. "And since this is the first one I've ever come across, I don't want to take no chances. My granddaddy told me 'bout ghost sickness, and he was a truth-tellin' man."

"Your granddaddy was superstitious, that's all," Peterson said, looking under the body.

Maurice shook his head. "That may be, but he said don't touch dead bodies and never be an undertaker."

"Look here," said the sheriff, holding up the dead man's wrist. "You see what I see?"

Maurice looked down. "I just see a dead man's wrist."

"Look closer. Lookee here," the sheriff said, pointing to the two red-splotched marks on the dead man's wrist.

"That looks like . . ." Maurice stammered.

"Like he was snake bit. I think it's a rattlesnake bite," the sheriff said, looking around.

Maurice looked around his feet. "Hope that snake's long gone."

Peterson stood up. "Maurice, let's look around and see if we can find it and I'll shoot it."

"I ain't goin' pokin' 'round for no rattler," Maurice said, shaking his head, " 'specially no killer rattler."

Peterson sighed. "You got long pants and boots on, so just keep your hands high. Don't reach down to places where you can't see and you'll be all right."

Maurice looked carefully around, high-stepping like he was marching in a band. "Wish I had me a horsehair rope," he mumbled.

"Why's that?" Peterson asked, carefully turning over a log.

" 'Cause a rattler won't cross a horsehair rope," Maurice said.

"Who told you that?"

"My daddy."

Peterson looked behind some rocks. "Well, your daddy was just playin' with you."

"I know you're right, but I can't help thinkin' 'bout what my daddy said with a killer rattler slippin' 'round here someplace."

Peterson looked behind a log. "Rope won't do you no good against a rattler."

"That's easy for you to say, 'cause you got the pistol," Maurice said.

"You want it?" Peterson asked, holding it up.

"All I know is that a pistol pointed at a rattler never misses, 'cause the snake aims its head."

"Maurice, those are just myths," Peterson laughed. "Even I know that."

"You just got here from Sweden, so you ain't had time to learn the truth and the ways. Snakes charm their prey, so that's why I'm only lookin' with one eye."

They both heard the horse. A tall man, dressed in black, was coming slowly down the road.

It was Jackson Rutherford, and he was seething that Brother Robert had not been more careful. *Leaving the body near the road was a serious mistake, one that will have to be dealt with,* Rutherford thought to himself.

"What's that you got there?" Rutherford called out. "Is that man hurt?"

"He's dead," Peterson said, eyeing the rider. He and Maurice walked back to stand over the body.

"Dead?" Rutherford exclaimed. "Who is it?" he asked, riding closer.

"Don't know," Peterson said, looking down at the body. "I was hopin' you could tell me. Man's got a thick red moustache and—"

"Thick red moustache?" Rutherford asked, interrupting.

"That's what I said," Peterson nodded.

Rutherford kicked the horse and trotted the last twenty yards, thinking to himself, *Act surprised, act surprised.* He dismounted and knelt beside the body. "Oh no."

"You know him?" Peterson asked.

"It's Brother Bill," Rutherford said, bowing his head.

"He's your brother?" Maurice asked.

Rutherford took off his black hat and closed his eyes, then looked at Maurice. "He's my spiritual brother, just as you are."

"What's his name?"

"His name is Bill Ponder," Rutherford sighed. "He was a good family man." He choked up, then composed himself. Sheriff Peterson looked to Maurice who shrugged.

Abruptly, Rutherford straightened up. "How did he die?"

Peterson picked up Brother Bill's wrist. "I think a rattler got him."

"Snake bit," Maurice added.

Rutherford looked closely. "Snake bit? He said he was going for a walk this morning and didn't return. How could this have happened?"

"Must have stumbled on a fat rattler sleepin' on a log or somethin'," Peterson said. He looked at the body and thought, *Something's strange. This body's bloated. Been dead longer than a couple of hours.*

"This is too early in the season for rattlers to be out," Maurice said, shaking his head.

Rutherford stood up and looked around. "It's never too early for the signs of life to lead."

Rutherford stared off into the woods, leaving the sheriff and Maurice looking at each other with questioning faces. Maurice rolled his eyes, indicating that Rutherford was a strange one.

"You said he was going for a walk," the sheriff said, straightening up. "He live with you?"

"Yes, he lived with me," Rutherford said, turning back around. "I have a small flock down the road."

"Flock . . . sheep?" Peterson asked.

"No. My flock of followers."

"What's your name, stranger?" Sheriff Peterson asked.

"My name's Jackson Rutherford, leader of the Flock of Life with Signs Leading." He stooped down and picked up the body. "I'm goin' to take Brother Bill home and bury him so his soul will rest in peace."

Sheriff Peterson was mesmerized by the intense man's eyes and didn't stop him. Rutherford hung the body over the saddle and turned to leave.

"Will you notify his next of kin?" Peterson called after him.

"I already have," Rutherford said, looking up. They watched him lead the horse away.

When Rutherford was out of hearing range, Maurice whistled softly. "Whooee. Glad I ain't in his flock. He looks like the big bad wolf himself."

Peterson nodded. "He acted as if he already knew what had happened."

"Well, your job is done on this one, Sheriff." Maurice looked around. "I best be gettin' home."

"This don't make sense," Peterson said, shaking his head. "I think I'll just nose around a bit."

Maurice got back up onto his wagon and shook his head. "Sheriff, some things in these hills are best left alone."

On the top of the hill, Rutherford stopped and looked back and saw Peterson staring up at him. The two men locked eyes, then Rutherford tipped his hat and continued on his way.

"As I said, Sheriff," Maurice said, turning the wagon around, "some things in these hills are best left alone."

CHAPTER 8

THE NEW RABBI

Rabbi Stern, it was good of you to come," Summers said, shaking hands.

"Thank you for the invitation," he said, rather formally, with his Russian accent.

The customers at Mom's Cafe and Laura were taken aback by the size of the rabbi. He was over six feet tall and thick as a bull. He looked at Laura, waiting to be introduced.

Summers looked at Laura. "I'm sorry, let me introduce you to Laura Ingalls Wilder. She writes for the newspaper and—"

The rabbi nodded. "I know," he smiled. "My good American friend Lev Wechter sent me wonderful articles you wrote about this Mansfield town."

Laura blushed. "I'm glad you liked them. Please sit down," she said, gesturing toward the chair.

They took their seats and Summers suddenly felt uncomfortable as they had already eaten. "Rabbi, would you like something, one of Hambone's special breakfasts?"

"I . . . I don't want any hambone . . . no, thank you," the rabbi stammered.

"Not eat a hambone. Hambone's the name of the cook," Summers said.

"I still would not want a man named Hambone touching my food."

"Oh, why's that?" Summers asked.

Laura helped the rabbi out. "That's because the rabbi is kosher and doesn't eat pork."

Summers blushed. "But it's just the man's name and—"

"I've already eaten. Thank you very much anyway," he said, folding his hands.

"How long have you been in America, Rabbi?" Laura asked.

"We left Odessa on fifth November of last year."

"Odessa? I thought you said you were from Russia?" Summers said.

"Odessa is city in Russia," replied Rabbi Stern.

"Why'd you leave?" Summers asked.

The rabbi moved his chair. "For two years we hide from the anti-Semites." He rubbed his eyes. "Every night the army came, trying to kill the Jews." He paused. "They massacred twelve hundred of my community. It was terrible . . . terrible."

The rabbi bowed his head and no one said anything until he looked up again. "They killed my mother, took away my father and uncles. We never heard from them no more."

Stern wiped his eyes, then continued. "That's why we hid. For two years. Nothing but nightmares."

He looked out the window. Laura and Summers sat silently. "I remember holding my son, trying to shield his ears from the screams. The root cellar was always dark. We shivered in the filthy, knee-deep water that poured in from the rains."

"What did you eat?" Laura asked quietly.

"Rats and grass," he said, closing his eyes as if to block out the memory. "At night, we Jews would sneak out, to gnaw on roots and tree bark. The soldiers would shoot the Jews who came to the market."

Summers whistled. "I'm surprised you didn't starve."

Stern nodded. "Many of my people did. My son got smallpox and not even the Jews would come near us. God spared my wife and I, but poor Abe was so weak and hungry."

He choked up for a moment, then continued. As he spoke, his Russian accent got heavier as he struggled to find the right words in English. "When I first saw your magnificent prairie with its sea of grass, it . . . it . . ." the Rabbi stammered. "It made me cry."

"Cry?" Laura asked. "Why did the prairie make you cry?"

"There was so much grass. When Abe was starving, I made up a child's game of who could eat the most grass. For days it was all we had to survive on."

Laura sipped her coffee. "You're lucky the smallpox didn't kill your son."

Stern nodded. "He's never regained his full health."

"Smallpox." Summers whistled. "I'm surprised they let him in."

Stern paused to cough into his handkerchief. "We were very worried and prayed throughout the trip. Then we heard passengers crying, 'There is Statue of Liberty!' " He smiled, thinking back on that moment.

"What'd it look like?" Summers asked. "I ain't never seen it."

Rabbi Stern smiled. "The most beautiful sight in whole world. I began to cry and knelt down on the deck and thanked God for bringing us safely here, away from Russia."

"And they let Abe in without any problems?" Laura asked.

"We were very worried, because others who'd had smallpox were put back on the boat. The doctor asked me if Abe had had the pox . . . and . . ." Stern looked down at the table. "I lied. I have asked God to forgive me, but I could not have lived if they had taken my little Abe from me."

"How'd you learn to speak English so good if you just got here in November?" Summers asked with curiosity.

Rabbi Stern laughed. "I was taught English by a group of American Jews who brought relief to our people in Odessa."

"Yiddle," Summers said absentmindedly.

"What?" Stern smiled.

Laura laughed. "He means Yiddish. It's just a joke about the printing machine of yours."

"I want her to see it!" Summers exclaimed. "It's as big as my office!"

"Not *that* big," laughed Rabbi Stern. "But it did fill an entire train car when we brought it from Brooklyn."

"Why bring the machine out here?" Summers asked, shaking his head. "Don't seem like there's enough Jews around here to print a one-page yearly, let alone a whole newspaper."

"Ah, but we Jews are scattered all over this prairie of yours. When they are handed a paper in the *mameh loshen* they—"

Summers interrupted. "The what?"

"The *mameh loshen,* the mother tongue. Yiddish."

"Are you going to build a synagogue here in Mansfield?" Laura asked.

The rabbi laughed. "It will be a while before we do that. Now, the Wechters and the Shapiros meet in my home."

Summers shrugged. "Rabbi, Mansfield's got a bit of everything else, so that yiddle machine—I mean that Yiddish machine—of yours will probably fit right in."

"We Jews have always fit into America," Rabbi Stern nodded. "It is a welcome land for us."

"America's a melting pot," Laura smiled.

"Before I came here," Stern said, "I thought it was an all-white, all-English country."

Laura looked around the room, listening to the accents from around the world. "We've got our native Indians, who were here to greet the Spanish, Africans, Portuguese, French, Dutch, and English when they came."

"Don't forget the Germans, French Huguenots, Scots, Irish, and Welsh," Summers said.

Laura nodded. "They've come from all over the world to make up America. The white-English myth came from their domination of the original thirteen colonies and their writing the history."

Summers sipped his coffee and nodded toward Laura. "Get old Laura Ingalls Wilder on a roll and there's no stopping her." Summers signaled for more coffee. "Well, it's good that you Jews have finally started comin' over here."

As Mom poured him more coffee, Stern smiled and said, "We've been with you since the beginning."

"What?" Summers said, choking on his coffee.

Stern, sensing some skepticism, nodded. "Mr. Summers, did you know Christopher Columbus's expedition was funded by two Jewish merchants and that the first white man to set foot on American soil in 1492 was Louis de Torres, a Jewish interpreter?"

"I've never heard that," Summers said.

"History is written by those who control the story," Laura said. "What I mean is, those who write the history books usually write about their own kind. That's why our books don't reflect what the black people or women have done for America, or about a Spanish Jew being the first white man on Columbus's voyage to set foot in America."

Stern sat back and smiled. "You have holiday called Thanksgiving. Maybe this year I teach children about the Jewish Pilgrim fathers."

The bell tinkled over the door. A pale, dark-haired boy, wearing a yarmulke, walked in.

Rabbi Stern stood up. "Mr. Andrew Summers, Mrs. Laura Wilder, I'd like to introduce you to my son, Abraham."

"Abe for short," smiled the boy.

Outside, a group of children raced by the cafe, whooping and hollering as they practiced for the big foot race.

"Are you going to enter the Founder's Day race?" Laura asked.

"Abe is still not well," Stern said, hoping to change the subject. Abe looked down, clearly embarrassed.

"Oh?" Laura said. "Have you taken him to see Dr. George?"

"No," the rabbi said, patting Abe's head. "We took him to doctor in New York. Said his lungs couldn't tolerate closed-in air. He said prairie would do him good."

"Well, we're going to throw our annual Apple Hill Farm get-together this Saturday, Abe, so you and your father will have to come."

"You are most kind," Stern said, bowing slightly. "But—"

"But nothing," Laura said. "We'll be serving fresh fruit and bread and if your wife would give me some of her recipes, I'll make sure there is some kosher food there for you."

The crash of a broken plate interrupted them. Hambone had the kitchen door open and had dropped a plate of grits and eggs.

"And I won't let Hambone touch any of the food," Laura laughed.

The bell above the door tinkled again. Sheriff Peterson walked in and sat at the counter. "I need a cup of coffee."

Mom walked over and poured him a cup. "Sheriff, you look like you've seen a ghost."

The sheriff took a sip, then cleared his throat. "Found a dead body out near the old Williams place."

Everyone in the room stopped talking.

"A body?" Summers asked loudly. "Who was it?"

"One of those new people from Georgia livin' in a group out in the old Williams place," Sheriff Peterson said.

"What was his name?" Summers asked, getting out his notepad.

"Man named Jackson Rutherford said the dead man's name was Brother Bill, Bill Ponder."

"Brother Bill?" Laura asked without thinking. "Did he have a thick red moustache?"

"Yup, he sure did," Summers asked. "You know him?"

Laura hesitated. "I think I met him last night when I was talking with Josie and—"

Hambone coughed and looked out from the kitchen. "Josie? You were out talkin' to that witch?"

Otis called out, "You were talkin' to a witch in the dark? Woman, you got guts."

"She's not a witch," Laura said defiantly. "She's just old and lives alone."

Peterson got off the stool and walked over. "I don't care if she's the good fairy. Tell me what you know about this dead Brother Bill and Jackson Rutherford."

All eyes were on Laura, which made her uncomfortable. "Just that Josie caught him hunting on her property and chased him away. He called her a witch and she called him a 'durn snake handler.' That's all."

The sheriff raised his eyebrows. "Snake handler you say?"

"Yes, snake handler. Why?"

Peterson looked her in the face. " 'Cause the man was snake bit. Rattler killed him."

CHAPTER 9

OLD SHOES

Terry looked at his father. "Why are you so interested in this widow woman?"

"She's just a friend whom I'd like you all to know better."

"She better not try to marry you," Sherry pouted.

"Why not?" Rev. Youngun asked, knowing he was losing control of the conversation.

" 'Cause Momma wouldn't want you havin' her over to the house," Sherry said, her eyes welling up.

"You're too old to be thinkin' 'bout girls," Larry said.

"Old?" Rev. Youngun smiled. "I'm only forty years old and—"

"And that's too old to be thinkin' 'bout girls," Terry said, interrupting his father. "Let her go find someone else. We like you just the way you are."

The conversation was going nowhere, so Rev. Youngun ended it. "Carla Pobst will be coming to dinner and that's that. You children will be on your best behavior—or else."

Getting up to serve second helpings, he thought he noticed something different on their feet. When he sat down, he looked under the breakfast table a second time. *I'm right. They all have their old shoes on.*

"Larry, how come you're wearing those old shoes? I thought you said they hurt your feet."

Larry squirmed in his seat. "They do, Pa."

"Then why are you wearing them?"

Terry jumped in to save the situation. " 'Cause we read about eatin' humble pie at school and—"

"What does that have to do with you children wearin' your old shoes?"

Larry looked to Terry, waiting for his brother to answer what he started.

" 'Cause these old shoes will make us know what it's like to be poor and not able to afford nice things," Terry said, with an angelic smile.

That was a sure signal that something was up. Rev. Youngun pushed his chair from the table. "I want you all to line up in front of me."

"Why, Pa?" Sherry asked.

"Just do it."

The Youngun children looked at each other, then slowly got up from the table. Their father eyeballed them closely.

"Sherry," he said, "I want you to tell me what's goin' on."

Terry squirmed and glared at his sister. *Pa always asks her first 'cause she's a squealer.*

"What, Pa?" she smiled.

"I want to know why you're wearin' your old shoes," Rev. Youngun asked, looking down at the ill-fitting shoes that had been donated to the church last fall.

" 'Cause I left 'em over at the—"

"We didn't want to tell you, Pa," Terry stammered, trying to steer the conversation, "but we took our shoes off to walk on the rocks in the ravine and couldn't find them in the dark."

"Do you remember where you left them, Larry?" Rev. Youngun asked.

Larry, who didn't want to lie, just told the truth without adding any details. "Yes."

"Where?" his father asked.

"Across the ravine," Larry said, fidgeting around.

"Can you be more exact?"

"We took them off near a big oak tree. It's a tree I'll never forget, Pa," Larry said, knowing this was enough truth to keep his conscience clear.

"Yeah," Terry added, "it's a tree that I could find blindfolded."

"But you couldn't find it in the dark?" his father asked, raising his eyebrows.

"We was so—"

"We were," Rev. Youngun corrected him.

"Yeah. We were so worried about gettin' home to dinner, that we thought it best to go back for our shoes after school today. That's why we're wearin' our old shoes. We didn't want to upset you none, that's all."

Rev. Youngun looked at his three scampsters. "But what shoes were you wearin' last night when they were all mud covered?"

"Feet shoes," Sherry giggled.

"What?" Rev. Youngun asked.

She giggled again. "We weren't wearin' shoes. Terry said we should cover our feet with brown mud and—"

"Hold it right there," Rev. Youngun said. "Terry," he sighed, looking directly at his auburn-haired son, "were you tryin' to trick me again?"

Terry put on an act of being offended. "Trick you, Pa? I was just play actin'."

"Play acting? Whatever are you talkin' about?"

Terry patted Larry on the back. "Larry read me a story about a boy surviving in the cold by coverin' himself with mud and leaves. My feet were kind of cold, so I thought—"

His father cut him off. "And so you thought that if you covered your feet with brown mud, I might not notice that you didn't have your shoes on and . . ." he looked at Larry, "am I about right?"

"Yes, Pa," Larry whispered.

Rev. Youngun looked at Terry. "Do you want me to finish it or do you want to?"

"You're doin' a good job, Pa," Sherry smiled.

"And so you put on your old shoes this morning, hopin' again that I wouldn't notice the switch." Rev. Youngun stopped and shook his head. "Terry, where do you get your ideas?"

"From you, Pa," Terry shrugged.

"From me?"

"It was in last Sunday's sermon," Terry nodded. "When you spoke about knowin' what wearin' the other man's clothes felt like."

Rev. Youngun shook his head. That had been his sermon, but he never intended for his children to use it against him.

"Terry Youngun, there's a difference between wearin' donated shoes and knowing what wearin' the other man's clothes feels like."

"What's the difference?" Terry asked. "Used shoes or used clothes, both belonged to someone else."

Looking at his pocket watch, Rev. Youngun pushed them toward the back door. "It's time to go to school. Just make sure that you go find your shoes on the way home. I don't want some dog to get them or some—"

Sherry wasn't thinking and interrupted. "Or a witch."

Rev. Youngun stopped. "Witch? What are you talkin' about?"

Terry was quick to respond. "She means a dog or mountain lion or whichever is worse, gettin' to our shoes."

Rev. Youngun wanted to pursue this new line of questioning, thinking something was up. "Sherry, is that what you meant?"

Larry knew what his father was thinking, and stepped toward the door. "Got to go to school, Pa. See you when we get home."

"Bye, Pa," Terry and Sherry said in unison.

He watched his three children scamper off down the road with Dangit the dog howling behind them. Beezer the parrot squawked about nothing, Crab Apple the mule hee-hawed from the barn, and Teddy Roosevelt the turkey gobbled up to the porch. Add to that the neighing of Lightnin' the horse and the grunts of Bessie the pig and it was no wonder that the Rev. Youngun was shaking his head.

"I just hope they don't all drive me crazy. Or drive Carla away," he mumbled to himself.

CHAPTER 10

BEST BUDDY

I hate these shoes," Larry said, looking down at the donated shoes. Ever since their pa had told them that the shoes had been left at the hotel by a group of traveling dancers, Larry had not liked wearing them.

Terry, who knew Larry was sensitive about his shiny, black shoes, shrugged. "Just pretend you're one of them dancers in leopardtards and—"

"That's leotards," Larry said, "and no, I won't pretend."

"Just tryin' to make you not feel as stupid as you look," Terry laughed.

There was something bulky in Terry's knapsack that Larry was curious about. "What you got in there?" Larry asked as they skipped along.

"Oh, just somethin' to help get our shoes back."

"What?" asked Sherry, all wide-eyed.

"I ain't tellin'," he said, trying to swat her rear. "But when I use it to get your shoes, you'll be thankin' me."

When they got to school, Sherry joined into a game of jumprope with the girls and Larry played catch with the bigger boys. Terry went looking for a way to earn some extra money so he could buy some candy on his way home.

He saw the perfect sucker. Sweet Tooth Martin, "Sweet" for

short. "Hey, Sweet," he called out to the overweight baker's son. "I got you a present."

"You did?" Sweet asked suspiciously. Terry never gave anything away without a string attached, and the string always seemed to be tied to whatever was in Sweet's pocket.

"Come on over here," Terry motioned, walking quickly behind the school.

When Sweet came around, Terry was looking carefully in all directions, as if someone might be watching.

"Where's my present?" Sweet asked.

"Hold on a minute," Terry said, shaking his head. "I risked my life to get somethin' for my best buddy."

Sweet, always a sucker for kind words and a sugar-coated doughnut, was flustered. "I didn't know I was your best buddy."

Terry nodded. "You're always there when I need you."

With one eye closed, Sweet asked, "What you need now?"

Terry ran his fingers through his hair, as if he was frazzled. "I need some money to buy some sugar. We're all out at home, 'cause I broke the sugar bowl."

"How'd you do that?" Sweet asked sympathetically.

"I was tryin' to fix some sweet tea for an old lady of the church, and when she screamed that she was goin' home to Jesus, why I jumped like a scared frog and dropped the bowl."

"Did your pa whup you?"

"Naw, he knew I was doin' a good deed. Only now we don't got any sugar. And you know that bein' servants of the Lord, why my pa don't make much money and—"

"You want me to lend you some money?" Sweet asked.

Terry, who didn't like to owe money, was flabbergasted. "I could never ask you to do that!"

"Then what did you call me behind the school for?"

Terry looked around, then whispered, "I got somethin' to sell you. Almost got kilt gettin' it."

Sweet's eyes went wide and round. "What is it?"

Terry held back his smile. In the past few months, he'd managed to sell Sweet a lot of things. Like some of Davey Crockett's hair, which was really a lock from his own head. And the prickly balls, which he'd convinced Sweet were porcupine eggs, and all the other tricks and woolies he'd pulled on him.

Sweet interrupted his pleasant thoughts. "I asked you what you got."

"I almost died gettin' this for my best buddy," he said, indignantly. He looked around again and whispered in Sweet's ear. "Before I show you what I want to sell you, I want to give you something. But you got to promise never to tell anyone where you got it."

"What is it?"

"Promise?" Terry asked, looking Sweet directly in the eye.

"I promise!" Sweet said, raising up his palm.

"Here it is," Terry said, reaching into his back pocket. He pulled out the straw that he'd gotten from Josie's broom.

"You want to give me some broom straw?" Sweet said in disgust.

Terry shook his head slowly. "Not just broom straw. Witch's broom straw."

Sweet's jaw dropped. "Witch's broom? Where'd you get it?"

Terry looked around and whispered, "You know the old witch named Josie who—"

Sweet interrupted him. "That old hag who lives in the holler and grows strange things?"

"The same one," Terry said nodding.

"What were you doin' up there?"

"I was up in the woods, tryin' to find a present for my best buddy," Terry sighed, patting Sweet on the back. "That was when I saw her landin' on her broom."

"You saw her land?"

"I swear," he said, putting his hand over his heart. "Cross my heart and hope to die. I saw her fly across the sky like a shooting star, then land on her porch. I snuck down and risked my life to get my best buddy this straw from her flyin' broom."

"Gosh," said Sweet, "you're a pal."

Terry put his arm around Sweet. "You're probably the only boy in Missouri who's got witch's broom straw," he said, handing it to Sweet.

Sweet grasped it like it was gold. "Thanks, Terry. I don't know how I'll ever repay you." Then he looked at Terry. "But you said you had somethin' to sell me. So how come you're givin' me the witch's broom straw?"

Terry nodded. "That's my gift to you." He reached into his pocket and took out the long strands of gray hair he'd tied in a knot. He carefully palmed it to increase the suspense.

"What I want to sell you is this."

As he opened his palm, Sweet fell back. "Is that . . . ?"

Terry nodded again. "Yup, it's some hair off that old witch's head."

"And you want to sell it? I bet it's worth a fortune."

Since Sweet usually had about two cents in his pocket, and gumdrops cost ten cents a pound, he was tryin to figure out two cents worth.

Terry looked at Sweet. "Seein's how you're my best buddy and how I need to get my poor old pa some more sugar, I was figurin' I sell it to you for two—"

Sweet cut him off. "I ain't got two bucks," he declared, reaching into his pocket. He brought out a handful of change. "All I got is ten cents."

"Sold!" said Terry.

CHAPTER 11

QUESTIONS

Sheriff Peterson had taken Laura for a walk to find out what she knew. Still, things just didn't add up in his mind.

He sat at his desk, trying to sort things out. *Why did Rutherford say the dead man had been gone only a few hours, when the body was so bloated? Why did Rutherford seem to be looking for the body when he came riding up to them?*

He decided to start at the beginning, so he mounted his horse and rode the back country trail to the Williams place. Mansfield was a quiet town. The only lawbreakers were an occasional speeder or Saturday night saloon troublemaker. Over the past weekend, he broke up two drunk farmhands fighting behind the saloon. One was hitting the other with a dead raccoon and didn't want to stop fighting, even after the sheriff had arrived. So he had to put all three of them in the pokey—the two drunks and the raccoon.

Sheriff Peterson rode to the spot where he'd found the body and searched around for any clues he might have missed. After a futile half hour, he headed up to the old Williams place, arriving just as the last shovelful of dirt was being patted on the grave.

"And we will all miss Brother Bill, won't we?" Rutherford asked his flock.

"Amen," they answered with varying intensity.

"Then let this be a lesson to you about obeying the laws of the

Flock. Each of you—" Rutherford stopped, seeing the sheriff standing by the edge of the barn.

Some of the mourners sensed something and turned. Rutherford continued, but changed the message.

"Let each of you be careful walking in these woods. Brother Bill was bitten by a snake, so each of you watch your step."

When the service ended, Sheriff Peterson walked up. "Mr. Rutherford, I'd like to ask you a few questions."

"This is not a good time to be talking, Sheriff. We just buried a Brother."

Peterson nodded. "I'll only be a minute. You told me that Brother Bill had gone for a walk, yet I heard this morning that you had sent him out hunting."

"That's right," Rutherford sighed. "We are a very poor flock and take our sustenance from God's animals in the woods."

"Then where was his rifle?"

"That was last night. Pity he didn't take it with him this morning," Rutherford said.

Peterson looked at Rutherford. *The man died last night. Rutherford's hidin' something.* "Mr. Rutherford, there's something else I heard."

Rutherford eyed him. "Tell me."

"I also heard he was huntin' on old Josie's property, and that she drove him away."

Rutherford's glare was piercing. "She's a witch, Sheriff. She put an evil spell on him which killed him."

"He was snake bit; that's how he died."

"Evil comes in many forms," Rutherford said slowly. "Everyone should watch out for the boundaries they cross."

Suddenly, Susan Ponder pushed open the barn door and ran toward Rutherford screaming, "Why did you cleanse my husband?"

Rutherford grabbed her in his arms and pushed her back toward Brother Robert. "Keep her inside," he shouted.

"It was your husband who died?" Peterson asked.

"Yes . . . yes, he was cleansed. Judgment . . ." She stammered, breaking down, sobbing.

"She's distraught, Sheriff," Rutherford said. "Take her back to quarters," he commanded one of the Flock.

Sheriff Peterson watched, thinking, *That woman has something to say. Think I'll come back later and try to talk with her.*

Rutherford cleared his throat. "Is there anything else?"

Peterson took off his hat and looked at the members of the Flock who were huddling in the shadow of the barn. "What'd she mean about cleansing?"

"I cleansed his body of sin when we buried him. It is part of our way. She thought he wasn't worthy and is just upset with grief."

"I also heard that Josie called that woman's husband a 'snake handler.' That mean anythin' to you?"

"Sheriff," Rutherford laughed, "witches say anything to confuse and mislead good people. The prayers of the righteous sound like screams to the evil ones."

"I'm askin' if it means anything to you."

Rutherford looked at Peterson and said in a deep, quiet voice. "Go ask the witch. That's where the answer lies."

CHAPTER 12

MORE QUESTIONS

Sheriff Peterson trudged across the ridge and looked down on Josie's cabin. A shiver went up his spin. *Even the sheriff can get the willies,* he laughed to himself.

He'd seen Josie in town, but this was the first time he'd ever been near her home. As he walked through the woods, seeing shapes in the shadows, he was upset with himself. He'd been brought up on the tales about the singers at the world's dawn. About Steadfast, the wizard, and his adventures sailing the seas in his copper boat. He'd tried to leave his superstitious upbringing behind in Sweden, but it all came back.

Peterson knew that there was no real place called Death's River, or Land of the Dead, but it was still hard to shake loose the tales he'd learned by the fireside. He shivered, thinking back on those cold, dark Swedish nights, when he cowered under his mother's blanket at the tales of the world of darkness.

It wasn't that he was worried about meeting Josie, whom Rutherford had called a witch. It was that in the boyhood tales he'd heard, wizards and witches could transform themselves into anything. They could be anybody.

Their magic was all powerful and could charm the wary and trick the unsuspecting. The sorceress could concoct brews to turn good people into demons.

He closed his eyes and shivered again. The tale of the sorceress came back to him—Sorceress Ceridwen, who pursued a young boy in animal form and ate him, then gave birth to the same boy as a wizard.

Peterson crossed himself and said an old Cornish prayer to ward off the fiendish forms of wizards and demons. To the shadows between the trees, he said:

> "From ghoulies and ghosties and long-leggety beasties,
> And things that go bump in the night,
> Good Lord, deliver us."

From behind him came a screechy voice. "Who you talkin' to?"

Peterson spun around, grabbing his heart. "You scared me!"

Josie stepped out with a basket full of herbs. "Don't go havin' a heart attack on me. I don't have all my herbs in yet."

"I . . . I just thought you were down there and—"

Josie interrupted. "And I'm up here, so what can I do for you, Sheriff?"

"You startled me."

"You deserve it for comin' on my property without askin'."

Josie looked at him closely. "You are a big Swede, ain't ya? Yes sir, that's why they made you sheriff," she said, walking around him.

Peterson blushed. "I was the biggest boy in my school."

"And not scared of the dark woods, are you, big boy?" Josie giggled.

"No, I was just—"

Josie cut him off. "You were just worried about ghoulies and ghosties and what was it?" she asked him.

"Long-leggety beasties," Peterson said, blushing. "It's an old Cornish prayer that I learned in Sweden."

Josie noticed the way he was eyeing her warily. "You worried about somethin', Sheriff?"

"No . . . no . . . it's just . . ."

"It's all right," Josie said, holding up her hand. "I've gotten used to people starin' at me."

Even when she tried to smile, her face was not a pleasing sight. Wrinkled, dimpled, her ugly chin warts with thick black hairs made smiling hard for Josie—and she knew it.

She'd been chased and made fun of for as long as she could remember. That's why she lived alone and kept to herself, helping only those who sought her out.

"You Swedes are all superstitious, ain't ya?" Josie asked.

"Well, I heard the tales when I was young."

"I heard 'em too," Josie laughed. "I know all about how that old archbishop of yours said that no one should risk a venture or business without first consulting a wizard."

"That's what we were told back in the village," Peterson said nodding.

"Ah-huh," Josie said. "And you were probably raised believing that wizards could find clues about the future from running rabbits and reindeer. Ain't that so?"

Peterson nodded.

Josie cackled. "And since you were taught that wizards could read the future from jumpin' fish and flyin' birds, that's why you're so nervous standin' here."

Peterson stared.

"You've heard people say I'm a witch, haven't ya? And all those tales you heard as a small boy are comin' back to you, ain't they?"

Peterson nodded.

"Well, take it easy, Sheriff, 'cause I'm no witch." Josie cackled so loud it echoed through the ravines. "You believe me, don't ya?

"I'm sorry, it was just—"

"You don't have to explain a thing, Sheriff. But you got to hurry, 'cause I got to go into the woods to hunt for fresh herbs."

The sheriff cleared his throat. "Ah, Josie Tatum, I came up here to ask you about a man you caught huntin' on your property yesterday."

Josie spun around. "Did that varmit come complain to you? You take me to him and I'll give him a piece of my mind." She huffed off down the trail. "Those snake handlers have gone too far."

"He's dead."

Josie stopped and turned. "Dead? What happened?"

"That's what I'm tryin' to find out," Peterson said.

"What you comin' 'round here for?" Josie asked. "Go down and talk with that Rutherford man. That's where that hunter lived."

"I was just down speakin' with him," Peterson said, looking her in the eyes. "He says that I should talk with you."

"Me? Laura Ingalls Wilder was here with me when I run him off. Go ask her."

"She told me about it. I ain't here accusin' you of anythin', just need some questions answered."

"Thought you were goin' to ruin my day," Josie said, sighing with relief. "Well, you can ask me the questions while I go into my garden."

Peterson looked down at the gardens below. "But your gardens are down there."

"Mother Nature is my garden," Josie laughed. "Come on, I'll teach you a few things." She walked a few feet and stopped. "This is my medical tree," she said, pulling at a branch.

Peterson looked at the leaves. "This is a wild cherry tree."

"Right. I make cough syrup from the bark. It helps the heart, too."

"But I want to ask you about the man who died."

"We'll get to that," she laughed. She bent down and picked from around her feet. "People call these dandelions weeds, but I make a medicine out of the roots that's good for kidney trouble. Same with the plantain broadleaf growing over by those rocks."

It took an hour touring Josie's living pharmacy before she began to answer his questions. For Sheriff Peterson, it was an hour well spent, putting the demons and ghosts of his childhood to rest.

"Now you ready to talk about snakes?" Josie asked.

Peterson nodded. "I want to know more about handling snakes."

"Okay, lesson one. Reach down," she said.

"What?" Peterson asked, looking down. There was a snake in front of his boots.

"It's a copperhead," she said. "Just back up slowly and you won't get bit."

The Sheriff inched backward and the snake slithered away. "I could have been killed."

"Just don't go surprisin' most snakes and you got nothin' to worry about." Josie looked up into the trees above them.

"What are you lookin' at?" the sheriff asked.

"Rattlesnakes can climb trees. I was just lookin' to see if there were any about to drop on your head."

The sheriff moved in a small circle, nervously eyeing the limbs above his head. Josie reached over and tapped him on the shoulder, shouting, "Watch out!" The sheriff jumped with fright.

Josie began laughing, but the Sheriff wasn't happy. "You scared me."

"I'm sorry," she said, through tears in her eyes, "but you were actin' like a scaredy cat."

"What'd you expect? Tellin' me that there were rattlers hangin' from the trees."

"Oh, Sheriff, I was just funnin' with you a bit."

Straightening out his shirt, he asked, "What do you think happened to that hunter?"

Josie looked into Peterson's eyes. "You handle snakes and you're gonna get bit."

"I don't understand. Handle snakes? Why? For what reason?"

"I don't much care which way or other a person wants to pray. But handling snakes ain't no Sunday church picnic."

"Rutherford said the man got snake bit out walking."

Josie shivered. "Maybe walkin' inside that barn."

"Have you seen anything you're not tellin' me?"

"All I'll say is there's things you wouldn't believe goin' on in that barn," Josie said.

CHAPTER 13

THE YIDDLE MACHINE

The noise from the three-thousand-pound clattering machine was deafening. Laura watched the Yiddish Linotype machine spit out the lines of type the rabbi was typing on the keyboard.

Laura was amazed at the gears, power belts, and pulleys, all working and clanging together. Stern was typing as fast as he could, and lines of solid type were coming out almost as fast.

He shut the machine down and took a line of type over to his assistant, who blocked and blotted it on ink and paper. Stern nodded at the headline he'd printed and handed it to Laura.

"What's it say?" she said, looking at the strange Yiddish letters.

Stern traced his finger over it from right to left. "It says, 'Jews from Around the World Coming to America.' "

"Can I keep this?" Laura smiled.

"I made for you," Stern said. "Come, let's go into house where we can sit and have tea. I'll tell you why we come to Mansfield."

At the barn door, Stern stopped. "Have you heard more about . . . about . . ." He searched for the right English word. ". . . about body Sheriff found . . . yes?" Stern asked, unsure of his English.

"I told him what I knew, which wasn't much."

"It made me think of Russia. We find bodies in morning after troops left. Every knock on door was . . . was . . . frightening."

"Rabbi," Laura said, "this isn't Russia. There aren't any troops that are going to come knocking on your door."

"I pray not," Stern said, "or we have come one halfway round world for nothing."

Laura and the rabbi walked on toward the house. Groups of children were outside, practicing for the race. Stern's son Abe was sitting on the porch steps, wearing his yarmulke, watching them. He began coughing, which subsided in a moment.

"Is Abe going to enter the race?" Laura asked softly.

"How I wish he could," Stern said, shaking his head. "But his chest, it coughs. He coughs so bad."

"Maybe he's allergic to something," Laura said.

"Only God knows. Since smallpox he has not been same," Rabbi Stern said, shaking his head.

"Does he wear his yarmulke all the time?" she asked. The rabbi nodded. "Do you wear one?" she asked cautiously.

The rabbi lifted his hat. Underneath was a yarmulke. Laura smiled. "I didn't know."

"It's part of our religion."

"Are they all the same? I mean, are they all black?" Laura asked.

"No, some white. But main thing is head should be covered." Stern could tell she wanted to ask more. "For two thousand years, it custom of Jewish men to cover heads, es . . . es . . . especially during prayer and study, to show God respect."

"Is he praying now?" Laura asked.

"Praying for friends, maybe yes?" the Rabbi smiled, trying to make light of things.

Barking dogs and clanging cans tied behind a car caught their attention. Sarah Bentley, married to the wealthiest man in town, came driving down the street, oblivious to it all.

Laura saw the smile on Abe's face. "These kids around here are rascals," she said laughing as they reached the house.

"I'd like to meet some . . . some rascals," Abe said sadly.

Rabbi Stern agreed. "He needs friends, boys, girls his age to play games with."

"What about Zeke Wechter? Isn't he about Abe's age?"

"He is gone now," Abe said. "Went with his father to sell rugs in Springfield."

"There must be other children you can meet to play with," Laura said.

"The only other Jewish families in the county are very old and have no children," the rabbi said sadly.

Laura shrugged. "Why do you want him to only play with Jewish children?"

Rabbi Stern sighed. "Before leaving New York, we read stories of how Jews weren't welcome in the West."

"Oh, Rabbi, people are friendly to those who are friendly back."

"But—"

"But nothing," Laura said, shaking her head. "Mansfield's got Catholics, Baptists, Methodists, Lutherans, Mormons, and . . . let's see what else. Oh yes, we've got African Methodist Episcopals, Congregationalists, some who believe part-time, some who don't believe at all, and a whole lot of in-between."

Rabbi Stern considered this and nodded. Laura continued, "I think that Mansfield's about as welcoming a place as you could find."

"We *have* been made welcome here," Stern said, nodding. "It's not what I expected."

"I'm glad to hear that."

Stern opened the front door. "Please, come inside. I want tell you how we came to this," he used a Russian word, then smiled. "Sorry, sometimes I mix up words. I want to show you what brought us to these Oz . . . Oz . . ."

"Ozarks," Laura said helpfully.

"Yes, Ozarks. Come, please step in my home."

Inside he handed Laura an article she'd written last year for the

Mansfield Monitor. "Lev Wechter sent this. It why we come to town," he said.

Laura took the article about life in the country she'd written:

COME TO MANSFIELD!
By Laura Ingalls Wilder

If you are seeking a freer, healthier, happier life, then come to Mansfield. If you are tired of noise and dirt, bad air and the rude crowds of the city, then turn your eyes to the Ozarks! Come to where there are green slopes, wooded hills, pure running water, and the health-giving breezes of the country.

Come to Mansfield!

We have the whole outdoors for our backyard. We are surrounded by beautiful flowers, grand old trees, beautiful birds, sunshine, fresh air, and wild, free, beautiful things.

The children, instead of playing in a city street or alley, can make friends with the birds on their nests or singing from the bushes. The children of the Ozarks are healthy. Instead of getting into trouble, they can gather berries in the garden and nuts in the woods, and grow strong and healthy, with rosy cheeks and bright, shiny eyes.

"That is why we come to Mansfield," Rabbi Stern said. "For health, Abe's health. So he could forget death and destruction of Russia . . . and be a child again."

CHAPTER 14

ANGEL?

The temperature in the Ozarks that afternoon was in the 90's, but without any breeze. It was a stifling day. It was even hot in the shade.

Josie had been gathering wild herbs from the woods to replenish what she'd used up during the winter on her patients. She called the woods nature's pharmacy, and spent hours combing the hills for just the right plants.

The visit by the sheriff had worn her out—all those questions about the snake handlers and what she knew about them.

She was tired and wanted some Ozark tea, but wasn't sure what kind. Back on her shelves she had horsemint, calamint, yarrow, catnip, horehound, spearmint, pennyroyal, goldenrod, chamomile, peppermint—there were so many choices that it tired her thinking about it.

Walking into the middle of her largest herb garden, she bent down and sniffed. "Think I'll have me some peppermint tea, that's what I need," she said to the bees buzzing around her.

Catching the sound of slow-moving feet, she looked up. "Tom Tamus, what you want now?"

"Josie, I been feelin' poorly," said the old man.

She looked up from her herb garden. "You been drinkin' the sassafras tea I made for you?"

"Yes ma'am, but I still don't feel like doin' nothin'."

Josie stood up. "I made that up special for you. It'll tone your muscles, help your skin, and I added some things in to give you energy."

"I didn't like the taste, so I mixed in some 100-proof whiskey."

"That don't mix with sassafras," Josie said, cutting him off.

"But—"

Josie picked up her basket and walked back toward her cabin. "Your blood needs purifyin'."

The old man's eyes went wide. "I went to church last Sunday."

"This ain't got nothin' to do with church. I'm talkin' 'bout gettin' your blood pure as nature intended it to be."

"You ain't talkin' 'bout puttin' no leeches on me, are you?"

Josie's laugh echoed through the ravine. "Leeches! You think you came to a hospital? I'm talkin' about gettin' your body to feel better without cuttin' you open."

"That's why I always come to you, Josie."

"When I was born in these parts, there weren't no doctors," Josie said. "Even if there'd been one, we wouldn't have gone. Nearest hospital was in Springfield, but that was fifteen hours away by buggy. So I was born at home, right here in this cabin."

"I was home-born too," the old man said, nodding.

"People like you been takin' all those liquor-filled patent medicines till your body's wore out. That's what's wrong with you."

"I stopped takin' those Brandreth Pills like you told me to."

"You bring me the bottle like I told you?"

The old man reached into his pocket and pulled it out. "Yup." He shook the bottle. "See, they's mostly still left."

Josie looked at the bottle and laughed. "Listen to this nonsense," Josie said, and read in a mocking tone, " 'Purifies the blood and cannot fail to cure. Second only to Christianity in the benefits it is capable of conferring upon mankind.' "

Josie looked up, shaking her head. "That's a lot of quack humdrum." She looked at Tom. "These pills do any good for you?"

"I think they stopped me up," the old man said, looking down.

Josie laughed. "I'll give you a jug of mineral water to take with you."

"How you stay so healthy?" the old man asked.

"I eat good. I beat the possums to the persimmons and blackberries for the vitamins and minerals. I eat the wild violet blossoms and get my greens from wild lettuce, dandelions, dock, purslane, and cattails. Mix them together and you got a better salad than any restaurant."

"You just know where to look."

"Come over here," she said. The old man followed. "Look at this greenbrier." Tom followed her finger to the bright green vine.

"This is the time of year to break off its shoots. Eat 'em raw and they taste just like asparagus."

Josie broke one off and handed it to Tom, who reluctantly chewed on it. She put some in her mouth and smiled. "Greenbrier's full of minerals, and it cleans your teeth and takes the stink out of your mouth."

Josie turned and didn't see Tom spit the shoots out. They walked past a heavy iron pot, simmering over a small fire.

"What's that?" Tom asked, sniffing the air.

"It's my base."

"Your what?" he asked.

"My base. I use it to mix with most of my prescriptions."

"What's in it?" he asked, eyeing the brown brew.

Josie shrugged. "A lot of things. Pure spring water, yarrow, hound's-tongue, wild peppermint, pennyroyal, some honey, and—"

Tom laughed. "Everything but the water pump."

Josie ignored his joke. "Taste it," she said, ladling him out some.

He sipped it with his eyes closed. "Tastes sweet!" he said, pleasantly surprised.

Josie smiled. "Pennyroyal's for everything from insect bites to fevers and convulsions. Yarrow's for colds and fevers, wild peppermint and hound's-tongue for headaches and stomach problems."

She turned around and headed toward her porch. The old man followed behind. "Can I come inside and watch how you make stuff?"

"Naw, you wait over in my visitin' area," she said, pointing to the two rockers sitting side by side on the porch. "Did you bring me any shoes?"

Tom looked down. "I only got the shoes on my feet, and they're about worn out and too small."

Josie looked at the man's threadbare clothes, then at his small shoes. The soles had popped loose in the front.

"Don't know if I want those shoes in my tree," she said, shaking her head.

"But I don't got no other shoes," he said, looking up.

Josie broke into a broad grin. "Well then, while I'm in here mixin' up some chickweed, dandelion, and burdock, I want you to go look in my tree."

"For what?" the man said, perplexed.

"To see if you can spot you a pair of small shoes that might fit you. I'll swap you shoes. That's what the tree's for."

The man looked over at the tall tree. "How am I goin' to get 'em down? I'm too old and weak to climb a tree."

"Oh heck, I'll climb up and get 'em," she smiled. "Then after you get your blood back to normal, you come back here and do some climbin' for some other poor old geezer."

The old man gave her a toothless smile. "You're a good woman, Josie. Maybe we ought to get married."

"Tom, you're eyesight must be failin'!"

"You're just an angel of mercy, that's what you are."

Josie laughed again. "Some people call me a witch."

"Josie, you've been keepin' me alive for years. I think you're my guardian angel."

"Angel!" Josie cackled. "I know I ain't no angel."

CHAPTER 15

SHOEHORN

"Durn right you're no angel. You're just a shoe thief," Terry whispered from his position behind the rocks.

"Shush, she'll hear you," Larry cautioned.

"How we gonna get our shoes back?" Sherry asked.

Terry took off his knapsack. "Got somethin' in here which should do it."

Larry said, "I been wonderin' all day what you got in there."

Terry pulled out a bugle and smiled. "I brought me a shoehorn."

"A shoehorn?" Larry said. "That's a bugle!"

"A horn's a horn." Terry smiled.

"What you gonna do with it?" Sherry whispered.

Terry ignored her, peering back over the rock. Josie was inside the cabin and an old man was looking up at the shoe tree.

"What's that old man doin' there?" Terry whispered.

"Lookin' at the shoe tree," Sherry said, very matter-of-factly.

Terry bopped her on the head. "I know that!"

"I think he's lookin' for shoes," Larry said.

"Better not want mine," Terry whispered, peeking over the edge of the rock.

Down below, Tom's eyes brightened. He looked down at his feet, then back up into the tree. Using his fingers as a measure, he tried to see if the shoes hanging above would fit his feet.

"Josie, I think I found me some!" he shouted.

Josie stuck her head out from the cabin. "That's good. I'll be right out."

The old man walked back to the cabin and sat in the rocker reserved for Josie's patients.

Terry pulled his head back. "Larry, you and Sherry go sneak to the shoe tree and climb up and get our shoes."

"What are you going to do?" asked Larry suspiciously.

Terry smiled. "I'm gonna sneak 'round the side of the porch and use my shoehorn to scare her if she sees you."

Larry and Sherry started out, but Larry stopped. "I thought shoehorns were for puttin' shoes on."

Terry winked. "This shoehorn's for keepin' the witch away from the shoe tree."

"Don't make sense," Larry said, frowning.

"Shoe trees don't make sense neither," Sherry said.

Larry and Sherry crawled through the bushes and got next to the big oak tree. Larry looked at his sister. "You stand down here and catch the shoes when I drop 'em."

"Don't drop 'em on my head."

"I'll try not to," Larry said, climbing up.

Meanwhile, Terry had sneaked around the other side and was flat against the side of the old cabin. The only sound was the creak of the rocker.

Terry watched old Tom rock back and forth. *Hope you're blind as a bat,* Terry thought. *Is he a goblin?* he wondered, looking for horns or a tail.

"You find you a pair of shoes, you said?" Josie called out.

"Sure did," the old man answered. "Not too high up, neither."

Josie came through the door. "While the herb tea is brewin', why don't you show me which ones you want."

Larry had dropped his and Sherry's shoes down. Terry's were just within reach, but there was no time. Josie was coming!

"Hide, quick," Larry said to Sherry.

She scampered into the bushes with the two pairs of shoes. Larry dropped down on the other side and lay flat behind an old log.

"Show me which ones," Josie said, looking up into the tree.

The old man pointed to Terry's shoes. "Them's the ones. Those right up there."

"Glad you didn't pick ones too high up," Josie said. She synched her belt tight, then pulled a pole with a hook from the bushes. "I always use this to pick out the low-hangin' ones," she said, and she hooked Terry's shoes and handed them to Tom.

"These sure do feel new," Tom smiled, slipping them on.

"Do they fit?"

"They sure do!" the old man exclaimed. "Can I have 'em?"

"I said you could pick out a pair. My word's my bond 'round these parts."

The old man tied up the laces. "These are the best shoes I've ever had," he said, looking down at Terry's shoes on his feet.

"Well, give me your old shoes, so I can throw 'em up in the shoe tree. Fair is fair."

Terry, worrying that Larry was still in the tree, stood up and blew the bugle. He didn't know how to play it, but he was able to make enough squeaks and bleats to attract attention.

"What in tarnation is that?" Josie asked. "Sounds like a pig givin' birth to a cow!"

Terry ran to the other side of the cabin and blew the bugle again. "Sounds like a lot of 'em," the old man mumbled.

Larry crawled over to where Sherry was. "Let's get ready to run," he whispered.

"What's Terry doin'?" Sherry asked.

"I think he's pullin' a Davy Crockett," Larry said, grinning.

"A what?"

Larry looked up as Josie and the old man ran toward the cabin. "I read him a story about how Davy Crockett tricked the Indians by makin' them think there was more than just him and his sidekick."

Terry threw a can and banged on the side of the cabin with a

stick. "We got you surrounded, you shoe thief!" He was starting to have fun, so he banged louder. "OK, men, everyone get your shoes back. We're takin' this shoe thief to jail."

Problem was, Terry hadn't kept track of where Josie was and didn't see her coming up behind him. "Yes sir, men," he shouted, "we're goin' to—"

Josie jumped forward and grabbed his arm. "And what are you goin' to do?"

Terry was caught off guard. "You better let go. There's a lot of men out there comin' to get you."

Josie looked around. "Ah-huh. Thought you could trick old Josie, didn't you?"

Terry caught his breath and gained some courage. "I want my shoes back. You got no right to keep 'em."

Josie realized she had a spunky kid on her hands, one who would probably keep coming back. "Look, Red," she said, "you show me which shoes are yours and I'll let you climb up and get 'em . . . if . . ."

"If what?" Terry asked suspiciously.

"If you leave me the shoes you got on your feet."

Terry looked down at his old shoes. "It's a deal!"

Josie let go of his arm. "Now, just show me which ones are yours and—"

The old man came round the back of the cabin and interrupted. "Everythin' okay, Josie?"

"Yeah, this rascal is goin' to show me which shoes are his."

"There they are!" Terry said, pointing to the old man's feet.

"Your shoes are in the tree, ain't they?" Josie asked.

"You threw 'em in the tree but they must have landed on his feet. They're mine. Give 'em to me."

"They're mine now," Tom said. "Josie gave 'em to me."

"Can't give what ain't yours!" Terry shouted, his eyes welling up with tears.

"Oh curses!" Josie exclaimed. "What a mess!"

Terry ran off around the cabin. "Don't be puttin' no curse on me, you shoe thief!"

At the front porch, out of sight, he saw the jar with the red lid. *That's what I need,* Terry thought, *so I can make something disappear!* He grabbed the jar and ran off.

Josie turned to the old man. "Give those shoes back."

"But you threw mine in the tree!"

"Pick another pair out," she sighed. "That boy will follow me to the grave until he gets his shoes back."

"Say, Josie," Tom said, "my muscles feels tight. You got anymore of that rub?"

"Got a jar on the porch. Might not smell good but it sure feels good."

Larry and Sherry caught up with Terry who had stopped at the top of the ridge. "What happened?" Larry asked.

"She gave my shoes to an old man and then she hexed me," Terry said, shaking his head.

"She what?" Sherry whispered.

Terry looked them both in the eyes. "She hexed me with her curses. But I took this," he said grinning. Then he pulled out Josie's jar of smelly rub, not the aloe vera rub she'd called her disappearing cream.

"Is that the stuff she used to fly on her broom?" Larry asked.

"Naw," Terry smiled, "this here jar is her disappearin' cream."

Larry opened it and sniffed it. "Phewhee! This stuff stinks." He held the jar for Sherry to sniff, but she turned away.

"Keep that stuff away from me," she said.

Terry winked at Larry. "Maybe I ought to put some on your face, you little squirt," Terry said, walking toward his sister.

Larry grabbed him. "How do you know you won't disappear if you put your finger in it?"

That was a good one. Terry was perplexed. "I think it only works on the person you want to disappear."

"What are you goin' to do with it?" Larry asked. "Put it on the teacher?"

"Hadn't thought 'bout makin' her disappear," Terry said, scratching his head. "I got it to help Pa out."

"How's that?" Larry asked.

"Just thought that we could rub some on that widow woman's face and make her disappear—keep her from tryin' to be our new momma."

The three Younguns brightened at the idea.

"What about your hex?" Sherry asked.

"What are you goin' to do?" Larry asked.

"Let's go ask Pa," Sherry said.

"Ask Pa?" Terry snapped. "I already told him a whopper about where we left our shoes and now we're goin' back without 'em and —" He looked down at their feet and noticed they were carrying their old shoes.

"Why didn't you get my shoes?" Terry asked Larry.

"I was reachin' for 'em when I heard her comin' toward the tree and—"

Terry spit and interrupted. "So you left my shoes up there and left me to try to save you both. That's a big, fat thanks for nothin'. I help you, you get your shoes, and all I get is hexed."

"We better take you to the doctor," Sherry said.

Terry wanted to bop her but held back. "Look, we can't go to the doctor to get a hex lifted."

"Where do you go?" Larry asked.

Terry scratched his head. "Only person I know who will know is Mr. Springer. Let's go," he said, stuffing the jar of disappearing cream back into his knapsack.

The Younguns took off across the ridge toward the Springers' farm.

CHAPTER 16

RUTHERFORD

Rutherford sat in the barn, alone in the dark. Things weren't going as he'd planned. Events weren't fulfilling the future he saw.

I've got everything and nothing, he thought. *I'm lonely.* There was no one to share his visions with, not the way he and his wife used to do. *She was a good woman,* he reflected. *She understood where the visions came from.*

Judgment's tail began to rattle from inside the crate beside him. "You hungry, boy?" The snake rattled louder. "You want me to find a big rat for you to eat? Or maybe a rabbit?"

The snake's head thumped against the top of the crate, rocking it back and forth.

"I wish you could talk, I really do," Rutherford mused. He reached in and lifted the snake out, stroking its head. "You understand me, don't you, Judgment?"

The big rattlesnake didn't move, except for its tongue which slowly crept out of its mouth, once, twice, three times. From the corner of his eye Rutherford saw a big rat standing frozen in the corner. He carefully put the snake down and watched as Judgment slithered along the wall.

Judgment's a hunter, yes he is, Rutherford thought, watching the snake coil to strike. With lightning speed, he sank his fangs into the rat, which squealed in agony. Then it was over and the snake slowly swallowed his prey.

Snakes. Rutherford picked up the snake and placed him back in the crate so he could digest the rat. *I remember when I first knew that snakes were special, that they were part of my vision.*

He thought back to Jonesboro, Georgia. Right after his wife died from the snake bite—from Judgment's bite.

They'd been walking together in the woods, talking about his visions. *She understood me. No one else has ever been as close.* He remembered that moment and cringed.

I was just telling her about my vision from the sunrise. How I'd seen that this day would bring changes. That God had chosen me, placed me on earth. That I was special, above all others, because He spoke only to me.

He couldn't block out the thought of his wife screaming, of one minute holding her hand and the next minute carrying her body. Running in the woods. Screaming for help.

The big snake had bitten her ankle as Rutherford stood there telling her about his vision. A snake had taken the only woman he'd ever loved. *A snake, a rat eater took her,* Rutherford thought.

For three days he wandered the woods, carrying the snake, trying to understand why God let it happen. He didn't eat or sleep, wanting to kill the snake and wanting to understand the reason why it had happened.

There was a reason for it all, he said to himself, over and over. And somewhere in the woods, he had a vision that the snake was part of the judging of all mankind. That the snake could show the signs. So he named him Judgment, and knew that it had come from inspiration.

Thus began his gathering together of the Flock of Life with Signs Leading—a group of believers who followed Rutherford in his life's mission. At first he had kept the snake to remind him how quickly life and love can be lost. Soon, however, he began revolving his life and the lives of those in the Flock around his belief that the snake could judge people and cleanse them of their evil.

Sometimes Rutherford would take Judgment with him to the

woods for several days at a time. And each time he returned, his followers could see that he had changed, that he had come back from the woods different—dangerously different, it seemed.

Eventually Rutherford began to see evil all around him. He read everything he could get his hands on about evil. He was particularly interested in the witches of Salem.

His Flock humored him at first, but his personal campaign to find and expose witches drove him like a man possessed. Strange-looking old men became wizards in his mind and old women who didn't agree with his visions became witches.

People in Jonesboro thought he was insane, with his rantings from street corners about the evil ones of the night who lurked everywhere.

He heard about a witch's market on the Georgia coast and went to investigate. When he saw the *Mercado de Brujas*—the Witches' Market—it was the turning point of his life.

As he walked among the stalls, hidden away from the main road, he knew he had found the Spanish descendants of Salem. Rutherford listened to a few self-professed witches selling herbs, curses, and good luck charms. He wanted to learn the ways of evil.

An old witch nodded to him. "Looking for a wife? I have just the charm for you," she said, rummaging through her knickknacks.

"No, I don't need a wife," he stammered, convinced they could read his mind.

"But you are lonely, no?"

"I am looking for something else."

The old witch laughed. "You have come to the right place. The witches' market is where dreams come true through the spirits." The old woman looked into his eyes. "Do you dream, *señor?*"

"Yes. I dream deeply, even when I'm awake," he nodded. "Where are you from, witch?"

She laughed to herself. "From? I am from the spirits."

"Where were you born?"

She laughed again. "I was born in La Paz, Bolivia. I am an

Aymara Indian. We believe that the other-world has the power to comfort and protect."

Rutherford looked at the old woman dressed in multilayered shirts, black shawl, and black bowler hat. "Why have you come here?"

She shrugged. "We go where the spirits take us. We have a lot of gods to appease. Have you protected yourself from the world above and the world below the earth?"

Rutherford just stared.

"Let me sell you something to protect you," she said, looking through her stacks of incense, herbs, and multicolored candles. "How about a special candle to burn with herbs to appease *Pachamama.*"

"Who?" Rutherford asked.

"*Pachamama.* Mother Earth. I have heard her called Mother Nature here," the old woman said.

Rutherford was dizzy. His mother had thanked Mother Nature for all her blessings. Was she a witch?

The old woman laughed, clapping her hands. "I can see it in your eyes," she shrieked. "*Brujas! Brujas,* come see," she shouted to the half-dozen old *brujas* in the stalls around her.

The witches came over and gathered behind her. She pointed to Rutherford's face. "Look into his eyes. Can you see it?"

The women whispered among themselves, then they began nodding their heads. "He's a *yatiri,* isn't he?" the old witch asked her friends.

Rutherford backed off a step. "A *yatiri?* What's that?"

They all began cackling. "A male witch," the old woman said. "That's what you are. Your eyes show the darkness of your soul."

"I am not a *yatiri.* I am not a witch!" Rutherford screamed.

"Oh, but you are *señor. Señor yatiri.*"

The witches reached out for him, wanting to touch him. "He is one of us," they chanted in unison, dancing around. Rutherford ran from the market, knocking over a table of burning, square candles.

As he ran, he saw the vision of what was happening. *The witches were trying to trick me. I was put on the earth to fight them and this was just a test, just a sign in my life.*

He stumbled through the brush, confusing the Old Testament with his visions and jumbled thoughts. "Scriptures teach death to blasphemers!" he screamed out. "Witches are blasphemers. They should all die. God will get them. I will get them."

Images of witches and broomsticks raced through his mind. The burnings at the stake in Salem. The torture. He saw himself standing on a cloud holding Judgment in his hand. Dressed in black, raising his hands, commanding evil away. Millions of people were at his feet, praying to him.

From that day on, he dressed in black and believed that he was special. That his visions were a gift. That the only way to cleanse evil away was through snakes, the sign he'd found in his wife's death.

Though he'd been bitten and come near death twice, Rutherford perfected his handling of the snake until it became a draw. His Flock was growing but there was grumbling over some of his bizarre visions.

Then came the night he was beaten by masked men on the outside of town. They told him to leave town. That snake handlers weren't wanted in Jonesboro. Rutherford told the Flock that the men were *yatiri,* sent to drive him away before he destroyed their evil power.

In the beating, too, Rutherford saw signs—and had another vision. He gathered those he deemed his most faithful and told them of his vision of the land in the middle of America, where the Flock could build their promised land.

But then came Josie, the herb woman. Rutherford remembered the witches' market and the herbs they used and sold. He became obsessed with driving her away.

Rutherford remembered it all as he sat brooding in the barn. In the stillness, watching the dust balls swirl when he moved his feet, he felt he could touch the silence.

I'm lonely, he reflected. *I've no one to be with. That's why I love the silence . . . the silence of it all.*

I wish it could last forever, this wonderful silence, Rutherford thought to himself. But then he heard the crying.

CHAPTER 17

SUSAN PONDER

Susan Ponder knelt down near the freshly dug grave. "Bill, why'd you bring us to this place?" she whispered.

She fingered the soil and touched the simple pile of rocks that formed the boundary. It seemed like nothing had gone right since they'd begun listening to Jackson Rutherford back in Jonesboro, Georgia.

Jonesboro, she thought. *So long ago.*

What had seemed so good, so right, had turned so sour. She and her husband were searching for truth. Trying to find meaning in the Scripture and make sense of the revival tents that always appeared out of nowhere on the edge of town and left when the money was gone.

Traveling ministers by the dozens came through, each claiming to speak the truth. But the messages were confusing. That's why Rutherford appealed to her and Bill in the beginning.

His message was simple: signs of life show the true way. It's what's in your heart and mind that bring salvation, not how others interpret things.

Rutherford was warm and giving. He fed the hungry and gave of himself. He was everything he preached until his wife was bitten by the big snake and died.

She thought of Judgment and shivered. *What would possess that man to praise the snake that killed his wife? No matter what he says, it doesn't make sense.*

Susan choked back her tears. Everything was worse now. Bill was dead, the children were depressed, and she was twenty-four, feeling fifty. She had no money, no horse or gun, and no real knowledge of where to find them.

With her head bowed over the grave, Susan whispered, "Bill, I can't stay. I gotta take the children and leave. Do you understand?"

The barn door opened and Rutherford walked out. "What are you doing, woman?"

"I'm praying."

"The man had evil. Don't be prayin' to evil."

Susan looked up and glared. "He wasn't evil. He was a good man," she snapped, then began sobbing uncontrollably.

"Come inside." When she didn't respond, Rutherford walked over and took her arm. "I told you to come inside."

"But I miss him," Susan said, breaking down in sobs.

Rutherford tried to comfort her. For a moment he was like the man she'd first believed in. "It will be all right, Susan. God will make everything better for you. I will do it for Him."

"I want to go home. I want to go back to Georgia. Please send me home," Susan sobbed.

"Don't you worry," Rutherford said, smoothing her hair. "I'll take care of you and the children."

"But I miss him so much," she said, holding on to his arm.

"The Flock will provide you with another man. You have my word."

Susan realized suddenly that *Rutherford* was the only single man in the Flock. She opened her eyes at the moment he kissed her cheek.

"I don't want another man. I want away from you and Judgment," she said coldly.

Rutherford slapped her and became the man in black again. "You'll do what I say, with who I say, when I say it. That is the way of the Flock. Do you understand?"

CHAPTER 18

DOUBLE DARE

Hey, Mr. Springer," the Younguns called out, running after the slow-moving wagon.

His wife, Eulla Mae, had told them Maurice was headed into town. So the Younguns cut across the field and caught up with him about a half-mile before the Willow Creek Bridge.

Maurice brought his team to a halt. "Whoa, steady girls." He looked at the Younguns. "You all want a ride?"

"Just want to ask you somethin'," Terry said.

"You got somethin' up your sleeve, don't ya?" Maurice said, eyeing Terry.

"Nope, nothin' up there," Terry said, rolling up his sleeves.

"What you want to talk about?" Maurice asked Larry.

"Just things," Larry said, shrugging.

Maurice was the adult the Younguns always took their questions and problems to. "Climb on up," he said, motioning to the back of the wagon. "I'm makin' a delivery in town, then I'll run you home. As a matter of fact, I got you all a present back at my farm."

"A present!" Sherry shouted, "What is it?"

"Is it a game?" Larry asked.

"Candy?" Terry asked.

"Naw, you think I'd waste my money on candy?" Maurice said.

Terry felt the money he'd gotten from Sweet in his pocket. In all the excitement over the shoe tree, he'd forgotten all about Bedal's General Store and the bag of gumdrops.

"You gonna stop in town for a bit?" Terry asked, now thinking really hard about the candy.

"Just long enough to drop off my load," Maurice said.

"What's the present?" Sherry asked again.

Maurice tousled her hair. "Girl, I ain't tellin' you. Just wait."

The Younguns snuggled down against the feed sacks, enjoying the afternoon sun. Larry whispered to Terry, "You gonna show Mr. Springer the jar of disappearin' cream?"

Terry shrugged. "Don't think so."

After they'd ridden past the Willow Creek Bridge, Terry asked, "You know anythin' about hexes, Mr. Springer?"

He turned and looked at Terry. "Hexes? You been readin' 'bout things you shouldn't be?"

"The witch put a hex on him!" Sherry said.

"Witch? Whoa, Nellie," he said to the horses. When the wagon came to a halt, he eyed them carefully. "What you kids been up to?"

"Do you believe in witches, Mr. Springer?" Larry asked.

"No, I don't," Maurice said, "but I do have an open mind. What you know 'bout witches, Larry?"

"Just that they ride brooms and—"

Sherry interrupted. "And she put a hex on Terry."

"Who did what?" Maurice asked.

"Josie. She put a hex on me," Terry said sadly, looking down.

"What'd you do to her?" Maurice asked.

"I didn't do nothin'."

"That'll be the day," Maurice said, shaking his head. He giddiyapped the horses forward. "You best tell me the whole story 'fore we get to town."

Larry began the story, stopping here and there to let Sherry and Terry add their two cents worth. "And that's what happened," Larry said, as they entered the city limits. He hadn't mentioned the jar of disappearing cream.

"What can I do about the hex?" Terry asked.

"First of all, folks say there ain't no such thing as witches. Second, just 'cause that old Josie looks like a witch don't mean she is a witch. You understand?"

The Younguns looked at each other. Larry turned and said, "I know that folks say witches aren't real, and if that be the case, then Josie ain't no witch. But we want to know what you think."

Maurice was in a fix. He was superstitious, even though he knew there was no real reason to be. He threw salt over his shoulder, avoided black cats, and wouldn't walk under an open ladder. It was just the way he was brought up. But he didn't want to worry the kids.

"I believe in bein' good and bein' careful," Maurice said. "Those two things will let you live a good life."

"But do you believe in witches?" Larry persisted.

Maurice shook his head.

"Do you believe in ghosts?" Sherry asked.

"Just the Holy Ghost," Maurice smiled.

"Not that kind of ghost," Terry said. "We're talkin' 'bout witches and goblins and ghosts."

Maurice needed time to think and saw that they were going by the town cemetery. "Hold your breath or you're the next to die," he said.

The Younguns turned and gulped. They tried to get him to move the horses faster, but Maurice just kept trotting along.

"Yes, sir," he said, holding back a chuckle. "No sense in bein' superstitious. No reason to hold your breath when you go past a graveyard or worry about haunts or what happens on Friday the 13th."

When they passed the end of the graveyard, the Younguns all exhaled at once. "What happens," panted Larry, trying to catch his breath, "on Friday the 13th?"

"Don't you know?" Maurice asked, trying not to laugh. "That's the unluckiest day of all."

"I ain't scared of those things," Larry bragged.

"Well, Mr. Brave Boy, then I dare you to walk through that graveyard in the dark, let a black cat cross your path, and go into that creepy haunted house, and go up to the attic and touch it on Friday the 13th."

"Touch *it?*" they all whispered in unison. They couldn't tell if Maurice was serious or just pulling their leg.

Maurice leaned over. "*It* is the rafter in the attic where Old Fred was hanged. You children want to take that dare?"

Sherry covered her eyes. "Look!" she pointed.

A black cat with a slash of white at its throat was standing in the road. It was a scrawny, pitiful creature, half-starved. It stared at them for a moment, then ran back toward the graveyard.

"What's that mark on his throat?" she asked.

Maurice was ready to burst out laughing, but kept on with the game. He was having fun scaring the kids.

"That is the very spot where the vampire bit it."

"The vampire?" they all asked.

"Lots of things come out at night," he whispered. "Sometimes people say they see Old Fred walking on a full-moon night, looking for his gold."

"Tell us about Old Fred, *please,*" Terry begged. Every small town has its haunts and ghost stories that are told to children after dark. In Mansfield, they scared the children with the story of Old Fred. It had been told to Maurice and almost every kid in town through the years, which was why Maurice was so shocked that the Younguns didn't know anything about it.

So Maurice told the grisly story about the man who lived alone behind the cemetery. About how Old Fred was rumored to have hidden a pile of gold in his house. And about the thief who hanged Old Fred from a rafter—but never found the gold.

"Did anybody ever find the money?" Terry asked.

Maurice shrugged. "Some people have hunted for it over the

years, but nothing was ever found. Now folks leave the house alone."

"What's so bad about touchin' the rafter where he was hanged?" Larry asked. "It's just wood, ain't it?"

"You kids don't seem to be scared of nothin'," Maurice said, smiling.

"That's right!" Terry said, puffing out his chest.

Maurice shook his head. "Don't be the first one in a line to show off. That's the one who usually gets in trouble," he counseled.

"It's just a story," Larry said. "We ain't scared of silly ghosts."

"So I guess you ain't scared to accept my dare to go in on Friday the 13th, in the dark," Maurice said in a low voice.

"You're darin' us?" Larry asked slowly.

"I don't like dares," Sherry whispered, closing her eyes, "especially ghost dares."

"I'm double darin' you," Maurice whispered back.

"Will you come with us?" Larry asked.

"Me? No sir!" Maurice exclaimed.

"But I thought you didn't believe in haunts and witches," Terry said.

"I don't," Maurice said, "but no sense in pressing your luck."

"What about the curse on Terry?" Larry asked.

"Ain't nothin' to worry 'bout as far as I'm concerned," Maurice said, guiding the wagon down Main Street.

"That's easy for you to say," Terry mumbled.

Maurice tousled his hair. "Since you don't know what kind of curse she put on you, and since you know that curses ain't real and that witches ain't real, why you got nothin' to worry 'bout."

He pulled up in front of the feed store. "Now, enough of these games. I was just funnin' with you, so don't be thinkin' 'bout goin' in that old house. You might step on a rusty nail or somethin' and get lockjaw."

"Lockjaw?" Terry said, perplexed. "What's that?"

Might be a blessing to my ears, Maurice thought for a second, then dismissed the thought as mean. "It comes from cuttin' yourself on rusty nails and knives. Now, let me get my business done. Then I'll be givin' you a lift home and get you kids your present."

"But what about the double dare," Larry asked. "Was that real?"

"Son, I thought we were kiddin' around. You forget 'bout all the double dare and witches talk. It'll just keep you up at night."

Maurice went inside the store, but Larry still wasn't convinced. "I think he was serious on his double dare."

"Don't talk about it," Sherry moaned. "I'm scared of Old Fred."

"What do you think, Terry?" Larry asked.

"I think I need to get some curse medicine," he said, jumping off the wagon without an explanation. When he turned the corner, he dashed into Bedal's General Store to spend Sweet's money. "Might as well get somethin' to make the curse feel better," he lamented to himself.

Mr. Bedal, the jolly French Canadian merchant, walked up behind the counter. "What can I get for you, Terry Youngun?"

"Got any specials?"

Mr. Bedal looked behind the counter. "Got Devil Treats, five for a penny, and some witch's pulls, and—"

Terry went white. "Naw, don't think I want none of that. How 'bout a dime's worth of gumdrops."

CHAPTER 19

ABE

be Stern sat on the front steps, his body weak from coughing. Since leaving Russia, his health hadn't been good.

His father thought he might have caught something else on the ship or when they were sleeping in the crowded dormitory in New York. "Everyone sick in this country," his father had said in exasperation after they got off the boat.

It was true. Immigrants were dying in the slums of New York. Disease and filthy conditions were allowing sickness to spread like wildfire. Getting out of New York to save Abe's health became his obsession. He wanted to distribute Jewish literature but his sponsors wanted him to stay in Brooklyn and help the new Jews from Eastern Europe adjust.

Menacham Shapiro, one of Mansfield's founders, had been an avid reader of the *Jewish Daily Appeal,* though the copies arrived weeks late. When he died, he left his house and estate to the paper, the only stipulation being that a paper for Jews of the prairie be printed with the money.

Rabbi Stern was hesitant, but then he saw a copy of the *Mansfield Monitor* and read Laura's article about life in the Ozarks. Lev Wechter sent it to him, trying to attract a rabbi to Wright County.

Stern was adamant about leaving the stifling city and was finally offered the Mansfield assignment. Printing Yiddish tracts for the

prairie Jews would not have been his first choice, but it was the only way to get Abe out of the city.

So Rabbi Stern, who didn't even know where Missouri was, left New York with his wife and son to head West. He only wanted his son's health to improve.

At first the country air had done Abe good. The fresh food and vegetables were a treat for a family used to dormitory cooking and ship's fare. Then the coughing started again and Abe found himself growing weaker by the day.

He wanted to play with the local children, but his father still was not used to the idea that non-Jews would welcome the chance to play with a Jew. The pogroms and beatings they suffered in Russia still haunted him. He thought it best that young Abe play with Jewish children, which was all right in Brooklyn. But in Mansfield, with the Wechters away doing business for six months in St. Louis, there were no other Jewish children around.

So Abe was left to read books and watch the world pass by from his front porch. The children of Mansfield seemed friendly enough, though he didn't understand the games they played. But he watched as carefully as he could, hoping to one day join in.

"Hey, kid," a voice called out, "what's your name?"

Startled, Abe looked around.

"I asked, what's your name and what's that thing on your head?"

Abe turned and saw an auburn-haired boy standing there. "What's *your* name?" Abe asked.

"Terry. Terry Youngun," he answered, stuffing another gumdrop in his mouth.

"What are you eating?" Abe asked.

"Gumdrops," Terry said. "I asked, what's your name?"

"My name is Abe Stern and this is a yarmulke on my head."

Terry walked up and sat down, eyeballing the little cap. "Oh, Zeke Wechter wears one too. You got to wear it all the time like he does?"

"I have to keep my head covered."

"Not doin' much good."

"What?" Abe asked.

"The yarkmul."

"Yarmulke," Abe corrected.

"Whatever it is, it's not coverin' your head. Wouldn't keep you warm in a snowstorm, much less a frosty mornin'."

"I'll have to tell that one to Father!" Abe said, laughing.

"Who's your pa?" Terry asked, holding out the bag of candy for Abe to take some.

Abe looked inside. He loved candy but didn't know if he should ask his father. "My father's Rabbi Stern."

Terry noticed him hesitate. "Don't you like candy?"

Abe shrugged. "Yes, but . . ."

"No buts, I'm offerin' you a free grab. Not often I do that. Not even for my sister."

"Then why me?" Abe asked, reaching into the bag.

"Somethin' 'bout you I like," Terry said, smiling.

Abe took two red ones and put one in his mouth. "Thanks."

Terry smiled. "My dad's Rev. Youngun of the Methodist Church, but we just call him Pa."

From inside the house, a voice boomed out, "Abe, who are you talking to?"

"To Terry, Father."

Terry heard the footsteps coming down the hall and saw Abe gulp down the candy. "Guess I better go," Terry said.

"No, please stay."

Rabbi Stern came out onto the porch and looked at Terry. "What are you doing here?"

"Just stopped by to say hello to the new kid and offer him some candy and—"

Rabbi Stern looked at Abe. "Did you eat any? You don't know if it's kosher."

Terry saw that Abe was in a fix and jumped in, with a quick wink.

"No sir, he said he didn't want to spoil his kosher. Said he had to ask you first. Right, Abe?"

"Right . . . Terry," Abe said, looking relieved.

Rabbi Stern sighed. He had come on too harshly. "What's your name, son?" he asked, sitting down on the steps.

Terry reached out his hand to shake. "My name is Terry Youngun."

"The minister's son?" the Rabbi asked.

"Yes, sir," Terry nodded.

Larry shouted from Maurice's wagon. "Terry, come on. We're goin' home."

"Gotta run. See ya, Abe," Terry shouted, running off.

Rabbi Stern looked at his son. "I know you want friends, Abe, but wait until health, your health, is better."

When his father closed the door, Abe began sucking on the gumdrop he'd kept in his hand. *I like that kid,* he thought.

CHAPTER 20

BACK TO SALEM?

Rutherford was on a roll. He had gathered the Flock into the barn to warn them about the evil that was lurking just outside.

"The school of witches has sent one of its students into the hills. An old one. Do you know who I am talking about?"

The Flock nodded.

Rutherford raised his hands. "Who is to blame for Brother Bill's passing? Is it you? Is it I?"

The Flock shook their heads.

He reached into the crate and pulled out the gigantic snake that had killed Bill. "Is it Judgment?" he asked, carrying the snake among them. "Is this snake to blame for followin' the signs?"

All eyes were on the deadly snake. Each person cringed as the thick brown head came near.

"Snakes are not evil; they do what comes naturally," he said, stroking the snake. "They just read the signs and act."

Rutherford peered through the slatted window, then closed it. "Witches are part of a shadowy sisterhood of the night. They can be beautiful or ugly, mothers, daughters, or sisters—even wives," he said, looking at Susan Ponder, who lowered her head.

"They can change the weather by stirring their caldrons. You might think they're stirring a pot of stew, but that pot's made up of people they've tricked and killed."

Now he had the attention of the Flock.

"Witches come in many forms, oh yes, they do," Rutherford said, as he walked among the Flock. "Even some animals help them. Rabbits in the woods are natural allies of witches. They are swift and can sit up and stand on two legs. That is not their normal way but was taught them by witches."

Rutherford looked around. "But snakes know the evil ones. They know the signs. That is why they eat rabbits and put their poison into the veins of those that are evil."

Rutherford put Judgment back into the crate and spun around. "Do you know that if you see a rabbit running down the street, that a fire is coming?" He looked around, nodding. "Oh, yes, I know the ways of witches because I have studied the books. We did not kill them all at Salem. Many escaped."

Rutherford looked across their faces, then paused, closing his eyes and tapping his staff slowly. He opened his left eye and looked around. "The men of faith knew who the witches were and pointed out 160 of them. But did they kill them all? No!" The Flock sat silent, hanging on his every word.

"They only hung five men and fourteen women. The rest were set free—free to slip away from Salem to breed again. And they continue to haunt us, even here in Mansfield."

Tapping his staff on the floor for attention, he raised his arms. "I am here to tell you that they fled from Salem as rabbits, as blackbirds and ravens."

Something bumped against the outside of the barn. Rutherford raised his hands for silence and crept to the window. Josie, hiding below the window, held her breath. She wanted to see what Rutherford was up to and was stunned by the insanity of his rantings.

Peering out and seeing nothing, Rutherford walked among his Flock, looking into their eyes. "Evil lurks just outside. Mark my words."

Josie's leg was cramped but she didn't move.

"I think we should take up the torches. Light will drive the evil away." The Flock got up to do as commanded, but then a large spider descended from the ceiling in front of his face. Rutherford took the spider by its own thread and walked it around.

"Do you know that spiders are the silent spies of witches? Oh yes, they hide in the witch's cloak and whisper what they've seen in her ear."

He dropped the spider to the ground and crushed it under his boot. "This spider will have no tale to tell. He won't be able to report back to that old witch, Josie."

Rutherford paused, took Judgment back out of the crate and held it over his head. In a deep voice he said, "That witch will never know that we are waiting for the sign to drive her back to Salem, to finish what should have been finished in 1692."

Josie slipped back from the crack in the barn. She had watched and heard it all. There was no way to stop what was coming. She could feel it in her soul.

My moment with Judgment is coming.

CHAPTER 21

BROOMSTICKS

Laura sat in her study, going through her books. Somewhere in her library was an account of the witch trials of Europe. Clara, the telephone operator, had called to ask how many witches there were around Mansfield.

"How many witches?" Laura had sputtered.

"I heard you know that witch Josie, so I thought—"

"Clara," Laura exclaimed, "Josie's not a witch and there aren't any witches in Mansfield."

"That's not what everybody's sayin'. I've been listenin' in on some of their calls."

"You shouldn't be eavesdropping."

"It gets kinda boring just sittin' here by your lonely so I just plug in every now and then to hear the gossip and . . . that's all."

"There aren't any witches. Tell that to the next person you listen to."

Laura found the book and sat down to read, trying to understand the superstitions about witches. She wanted to write an article about the silliness of such fears, so she could stop the whispers about Josie.

Reading through the afternoon, Laura finally put the book down and shook her head. She made herself a cup of coffee and began to write.

SO YOU BELIEVE IN WITCHES?
By Laura Ingalls Wilder

I have heard the whispers in town about witches and evil things in the night.

What has surprised me about the latest whispering is that it comes from the mouths of adults. Children have vivid imaginations and fear what they don't understand. But grown men and women should know better than to accuse Josie Tatum, the old woman of the hills, of being a witch, just because she's different.

While some jest about superstitions, black cats, and broomsticks, others are deadly serious. Before this talk of witches goes any further, let me give you a bit of history.

Over five hundred thousand people were convicted of witchcraft and burned to death in Europe in just two hundred years. That's like taking almost the entire population of Missouri and burning them at the stake.

Their crimes? They were accused of having pacts with the devil. The reality? They were the victims of ignorance and prejudice.

The evidence? "Confessions" the witches gave. The only problem was that the confessions were obtained through torture.

The whole bizarre witch craze that swept Europe, and was later brought to America, was bred from ignorance. It was a time when few people could read or write, and so relied on the word of others.

The ideas of witches' broomsticks and casting spells came from the mind of the witch burners, not the women they accused. What was true then is true now: ignorance breeds ignorance. There are no witches in Mansfield. But there are ignorant people.

Those who call Josie Tatum a witch might as well call me a witch. Just remember, we are not all cut from the same cloth.

Laura left the article in the kitchen, planning to think about it for the night before she submitted it for publication.

"You finish your article?" Manly asked when she came into the bedroom.

"I think so. I'm going to read it over tomorrow and if it still reads well, I'll take it to the newspaper in the morning."

"Just let me know," Manly said, slipping into his nightshirt. "'Cause I'm going to town to get some feed and I can take it in for you."

When Manly left for town the next morning, he thought he was doing Laura a favor and took it to the newspaper for her.

CHAPTER 22

BASHFUL

Y ou sure you don't have any more candy?" Larry asked, eyeing Terry.

"Nope," Terry said, shaking his head. "Had me three pieces, one for me, one for you, and one for nitwit," he said, nodding to Sherry.

"That's not nice. I'm tellin'!" she said.

"It ain't like you to just go givin' candy away," Larry said, frowning.

"I told you," Terry shrugged, "I thought that new boy was nice so I gave him yours."

Maurice pulled the wagon into his farm and the Younguns looked around. Terry thought about sneaking a gumdrop out of the bag hidden down in his underbritches, but was afraid they might see him.

"Where's our present?" Sherry asked.

"Maybe I'll just wait until tomorrow to give it to you," Maurice said, chuckling.

"Oh, please," Terry moaned. "I won't be able to sleep."

"Come on, Mr. Springer," Larry said, "you promised."

Maurice got down off the wagon and lifted Sherry from the bench seat. "Go look in the barn."

The Younguns dashed off with Larry leading the way. Inside the barn, they looked around, expecting to see something new and shiny—like a toy wagon or something.

"Ain't nothin' here," Terry said, with a disgruntled look on his face. "Maybe it's behind the stall here," he said, sneaking out of sight to eat a gumdrop as fast as he could.

Sherry peeked over the half-door. "What are you chewin'?"

Terry swallowed quickly. "Nothin'! Just chewin' on the question of where our present is."

Tethered in the middle of the barn was a small, black-and-white goat. Maurice came through the door and stood with his arms folded.

"You find it?" he asked, amused by their search.

"Give us a clue," said Larry.

"Okay," Maurice said, "it's about two-and-a-half feet tall."

The kids looked around. Terry climbed up into the hayloft. "Just hay and rats up here."

"Give us another hint," pleaded Sherry.

Maurice scratched his chin. "Let's see, it's about three feet long."

Sherry looked at the old milk cow. "This cow is bigger than three feet."

Larry smiled slyly. "You ain't pullin' a wooly on us, are you?"

"Me?" Maurice said, holding up his palms. "Why, I'm a foundin' member of the African Methodist Episcopal Church."

"Then give us another hint," Terry called from the loft.

Maurice closed his eyes. "Let's see. It's black and white."

Terry climbed down and looked at the goat. "The only thing black and white 'round here is this goat."

"You're welcome," Maurice said.

"For what?" Terry asked.

"That's your present."

The three Younguns surrounded the goat. The goat just looked at them.

"A goat?" Sherry exclaimed. "Who wants a goat?"

"This one's special," said Maurice quietly. "You know that the Bible says that the meek shall inherit the earth."

The Younguns nodded.

"Well, children, this is the meekest of God's creatures."

Larry eyed the goat who licked its face. "What's so meek about this goat?"

Terry laughed. "Goats eat cans and they butt heads with anythin'. They ain't meek."

Maurice smiled. "This one's meek all right. You'll see."

Terry thought Maurice was pulling one on them, so he went up behind the goat and shouted, "Boo!"

The goat fainted.

"It's dead!" Sherry screamed, hitting her brother. "You killed it!"

"I'm sorry. I didn't mean no harm," Terry cried, trying to revive the stiff goat.

"That's what I was tryin' to tell you," Maurice said, laughing at the children's reaction. "This here's a faintin' goat."

"A what?" Larry asked.

"I said, it's a faintin' goat. Every time you scare it or it gets to bein' afraid of somethin', why it just falls over."

"How long does it stay down?" Terry asked, rubbing the goat's head.

"'Bout a minute," Maurice said.

The goat began blinking his eyes and struggled to get back up.

"It takes 'bout another minute until their muscles loosen up and they can walk normal again."

"Does it do anythin' else besides faint?" Terry asked.

"Eat, sleep, and do its business like any other normal goat," Maurice smiled.

Larry rubbed the goat's head. "Where'd you get it?"

Maurice put his thumbs in his belt loops and grinned. "I was down in the south county area and came across a sheep man who was usin' these faintin' goats as sacrificial lambs."

"You mean a sacrificial goat, don't ya?" Larry asked.

"Naw, sacrificial lamb," Maurice said. "The old sheep farmer would leave one of these faintin' goats with his sheep so if a wolf struck, it would faint and the killer would eat the goat instead of the sheep."

Sherry petted the goat who licked her hand. "I don't want any mean old wolf to eat you," she whispered.

Maurice continued. "So I thought you kids would like to have him, so I bought him for you."

"Gosh, thanks, Mr. Springer," Larry said.

"You mean we get to keep it?" Terry beamed.

"It's yours to take home."

"Yippee!" Terry shouted, and the goat fainted again.

Maurice shook his head. *Maybe this is not the right gift for these three kids,* he thought to himself.

"You can't be doin' any loud shoutin' or spookin' 'round this goat," Maurice said, picking it up, "'cause otherwise he'll be doin' more faintin' than standin'." He laid the goat on his side.

When the goat came back around, Larry picked him up. "Come on, we better be gettin' this goat home."

"Thanks, Mr. Springer," Terry said.

"What are you goin' to name him?" Maurice asked.

"We're goin' to name him . . . Bashful," Sherry smiled.

"Bashful. I think that's a good name for him," Maurice smiled, crossing his fingers behind his back.

Getting Bashful home was another matter. Terry, who liked to scream and play jokes at the oddest moments, accidently made the goat faint three times.

At the house, Rev. Youngun leaned back in his chair. *I wish Carla was here,* he thought. *I wish she were with me every moment of the day.*

He daydreamed, thinking about their times together. Buggy riding. Holding hands. Secret glances. And kissing. It made him shiver, thinking about the softness of her lips when they held each other that special moment in Cape Girardeau.

I wish that moment could last forever. I wish she were in my arms right now. Married to me. Hugging me. Planning a future together. Helping me take care of the kids and—

Larry yelled, "Pa, come look what Mr. Springer gave us."

"What is it?" he said grumpily, not pleased to be awakened from such pleasant thoughts.

"Come see," said Sherry.

"Yeah, it's somethin' we've always needed," Terry added.

Looking out the front door, Rev. Youngun was *really* not pleased. "A goat? Where'd you get it?"

"Mr. Springer gave him to us," smiled Sherry. "His name is Bashful."

"We don't need another pet," Rev. Youngun said, shaking his head.

"But this goat's special!" Terry exclaimed.

Beezer the parrot walked out through Rev. Youngun's legs and eyed the goat.

"A goat's a goat," Rev. Youngun said. "You take it back to Mr. Springer right now. We don't need another pet around here."

"But Pa," Larry pleaded, "this goat's different."

"What's different about—"

Beezer squawked out, interrupting Rev. Youngun. "Say your prayers!"

Bashful fainted dead away. "What happened?" Rev. Youngun asked, thinking the goat had died.

"Pathetic!" Beezer squawked out.

"Hush up, Beezer!" Larry shouted, stroking Bashful's head.

"Is he dead?" Rev. Youngun asked quietly.

"Naw," Terry said, "he likes to do that."

"Do what?" Rev. Youngun asked.

"That," Sherry answered.

Larry nodded. "He's a faintin' goat, Pa. A rare faintin' goat."

"A fainting goat? I've never heard of such a thing," Rev. Youngun said.

Bashful blinked his eyes, then stretched out his legs, struggling to stand up.

"It takes him a moment to unfaint," Terry said.

"What good is a fainting goat?" Rev. Youngun asked.

"It's good for lots of things," Sherry said.

Rev. Youngun shook his head. "Like what?"

Terry jumped in. "Well, if a wolf comes into the yard to eat us, Bashful can faint and the wolf will eat him."

Rev. Youngun just stared.

Terry kept on. "And when we tell scary stories, Bashful can pretend to be scared of them."

Rev. Youngun just shook his head.

"And if you scream at us, Bashful will faint," Larry added.

Sherry shrugged. "And Bashful will teach us to be more quieter."

That got his attention. "You think so?"

"Certainly," Larry said. "'Cause if we run around screaming, Bashful will spend more time fainted than unfainted."

Rev. Youngun smiled. "There's no such word as unfainted."

Larry shrugged. "Whatever you call it after he wakes up, if we don't learn to be quieter, it'll be bad for Bashful."

Sherry reached out and hugged the goat. "And we love Bashful!"

"And that's the truth!" Terry screamed, clapping his hands loudly.

Bashful fainted and Larry bopped Terry. "See, you made him faint, big mouth!"

"I was just—"

Rev. Youngun interrupted them. "Maybe that goat will do some good. Might quiet you children down."

"Can we keep him, Pa?" they all said in unison.

Bashful struggled to stand up, blinking his eyes.

Rev. Youngun shook his head. "Find a place for Bashful in the barn and just be—"

"Yippeeeeeeee!" they all shouted, and Bashful fainted again.

"—quiet," Rev. Youngun said, shaking his head.

CHAPTER 23

OLD MAID OF THE MOUNTAINS

The next morning, Laura's phone wouldn't stop ringing. Everybody was calling about her article on witches.

Laura looked at Manly and shook her head. "Manly, you should ask me next time before you just go off taking one of my articles to the newspaper."

"Just thought I was doin' you a favor, that's all."

Laura had wanted to interview Josie for the article, but it was too late. Even though Josie kept to herself in the woods, Laura felt she should warn her about the article and explain the mishap. She had promised to return the lantern and cane anyway. She would use that as an excuse for coming. Somehow, she'd work in the article and take it from there.

So she set off to find Josie. Along the way she felt like someone was watching her. She wasn't sure, but she could feel something, somewhere.

Standing on the ridge above her were Rutherford and Brother Robert. Rutherford had been into town to get supplies and had read Laura's article. "Brother Robert," he said, shaking his head, "I think she's a witch."

"Are you sure?"

Rutherford nodded gravely. "She's consorting with a witch and defending her in town. Evil is as evil does."

"Then you have seen the signs?" Brother Robert asked.

"I have seen the signs."

Someone else was also watching Laura—and watching Rutherford. It was Susan Ponder.

She knew that Rutherford was marking the woman walking in the woods below them. Susan knew she had to warn this stranger.

Slipping down the ravine, Susan sneaked along next to Laura. She was waiting for a place to speak to Laura where Rutherford wouldn't be able to see her.

Laura had seen her coming but didn't know what to make of it. So she continued along, watching Susan out of the corner of her eye.

Finally, as she came to a small stream, she stopped and said without looking, "I know you're following me. Why?"

Susan stopped.

Laura turned. "You're right behind that tree. Come out where I can see you."

Susan peeked around the trunk of the tree. "He's watching you."

"Who?" Laura said.

"He's watching you from on top of the hill."

Laura looked up and saw a man in black standing beside a big burly man.

"Who is that?" Laura asked.

"He is the leader of the Flock, Jackson Rutherford," Susan said. "And that's Brother Robert."

Laura looked toward the tree. "Rutherford . . . the snake handler?"

"Yes," Susan answered softly, "the snake handler."

"Does he know you're following me? Did he send you?"

Susan's eyes gave the answer. "No. I wanted to warn you that he's marked you as a witch. He told the Flock this morning that he'd seen the signs."

"He probably saw the paper," Laura said, shaking her head.

"What?" Susan asked.

"Oh, nothing," Laura said. "What's your name?"

"Susan . . . Susan Ponder"

"My name is Laura Ingalls Wilder. Walk along with me and tell me about that man up there."

Susan shook her head. "I can't. If he sees me talkin' with you, I'll have to be cleansed."

"Cleansed?" Laura said. "What's that?"

"Snake cleansing. Like what happened to my husband."

"Your husband?" Laura gasped. "Was he the one they found dead on the road?"

Susan nodded. "That's where they put him. Now he's in the grave."

Laura looked perplexed. "I don't understand. What is this snake cleansing?"

Susan looked up toward the top of the hill. "I think he's comin'. I got to go."

"But tell me . . ."

It was too late. Laura watched Susan run through the shadowed woods like a deer. Moments later, she heard the crunch of leaves behind her and turned. It was Rutherford, dressed in black, holding his staff.

"Why are you following me?" Laura asked.

"Why are you going to consort with that witch?" Rutherford said, ignoring her question.

"You mean Josie Tatum? She's no witch!"

Rutherford closed his eyes and mumbled something, then looked at her. "Witches always lie. That is their nature."

"This is Mansfield, Missouri, not Salem, Massachusetts. And the year is 1906, not 1692," Laura said.

Rutherford shook his head. "I will not be swayed. Turn back if you're not evil," he said, stepping forward to block her path. "Accept the true way. Accept and follow me."

Laura walked around him. "If you don't mind, I'm going to be on my way. I'd appreciate your not following me."

"The signs are here," Rutherford said loudly. "I can read them."

"Maybe I should be puttin' me up a no trespassin' sign," Josie said, walking out of the bushes. "That's the only sign you need to be readin'."

Rutherford took a step back. "The evil one again."

Josie cackled. "In the flesh."

Holding up his staff, Rutherford cried out, "Protect us from the evil ones, the shapeless ones of the night. Keep the Flock cleansed so that we can follow the signs and the visions."

Josie spit and took the cane from Laura's hand. She pushed up against Rutherford. "I've heard about enough of your claptrap for one day. You git off my property."

Rutherford backed away. "I leave because the signs say that we will meet again—once and for all." He turned and walked into the shadows of the woods.

Laura shivered. "Nice man," she said sarcastically.

"There is a special burnin' place for people like him," Josie replied, spitting on the ground.

"I thought you didn't believe in religion."

Josie shrugged. "I don't follow tent preachers with their hands out and I don't like goin' to church. Don't mean that I don't know someone created us."

"Do you read the Bible?"

"I might just know your Good Book better than you," she said, smiling. Josie laughed and spun around, tapping her foot. "In Genesis, it says, 'I have given you every herb bearing seed, which is upon the face of all the earth, and every tree, in the which is the fruit of a tree yielding seed; to you it shall be for meat.'"

"I'm impressed," Laura said.

"There's more," Josie said, laughing. "In Ezekiel, it says, 'The fruit thereof shall be for meat, and the leaf thereof for medicine.'"

Josie took Laura by the hand. "Come on, walk back to the cabin with me for that visit you promised."

Along the way, Josie preached about living in harmony with nature. "One day people will realize that everything the body needs can be found in nature. It's all right here if you know where to look."

"Do you mind if I take some notes?" Laura asked, taking out her pad and pencil.

"You writin' an article on me?" Josie winked.

"Thinking about it." Laura winked back.

Josie laughed. "Go ahead. Write what you want. Just don't call me a witch or a gypsy. That's all I ask."

With her cane, Josie led Laura through her natural world. "Did you know that Mother Nature has a fruit, herb, or vegetable for practically everythin' that ails us? Why, grazing animals, you've seen 'em goin' to eat things when they're feelin' poorly. Even dogs will eat grass when their body tells 'em they need it."

Josie stopped and shook her head. "But what have we done with nature's cravin's for healin'? Why, we go eat candy or ice cream or take medicine with God-knows-what in it."

"Is all medicine bad?" Laura asked.

"No, but most people take it when they don't need it." Josie tapped her stomach. "The body is like someone speakin' from a podium. It tells you what you need when you got the miseries if you'll only listen."

"You mean like 'an apple a day'?"

"Takin' care of yourself is just that simple. It might not always be an apple a day, but it might be beet juice, or takin' a walk to relax and eatin' healthy."

"Show me some things you'd pick around here."

Josie plodded along looking around. "Here's my patch of violets," she said pointing to the flowers. "I make a tea from their leaves that purifies the blood."

"Really?" Laura said, fascinated.

"And I use the roots from that yellow dock over there for the same thing, depending if there are any violets 'round or not."

Across another stream, Josie stopped. "That husband of yours. He limps, don't he?"

"Ever since the stroke he suffered back in the Dakotas."

Josie squinted her eyes in thought. "He needs the roots of the poke over by them big trees over there," she said, pointing to a ten-foot-tall, thick, bushy plant. "Those roots are good medicine for arthritis. If you boil it with a touch of yellow dock, why my patients say drinkin' it takes away the pain and stiffness. You want me to make you up some for that husband of yours?"

"I don't want to put you to any trouble."

"Just 'cause I'm old and ugly, don't mean I don't know 'bout these woods. You got any warts?"

Laura, looking at the two big ones on Josie's face, shook her head.

"Well, for warts, I take that wild lettuce growing over there and squeeze out its white milk. Put that on a wart and sometimes it makes it fall off. Didn't work on mine." Josie laughed, scratching the two on her face. "But it's helped others."

Stopping by a tree with bees buzzing around, Josie turned to Laura. "Want some fresh honey?"

"Oh, no. I don't want to get stung."

"You usually don't get stung if you're careful and quick," she said, as she reached her hand into the trunk of the tree.

Laura watched, amazed at her courage. Josie's arm was covered by bees—like a thick, moving shirt—but none of them stung her.

Laura had seen her Pa do this back on the prairie, taking out the honeycombs so they'd have something to sweeten their cakes. Josie pulled out a large honeycomb and slowly shook her arms until the bees flew off.

"Don't you want some?" Josie asked, licking her fingers.

"No. I'm not really hungry," Laura said, watching the bees slowly depart.

"People been usin' honey for remedies since the beginning of time. It's filled with good things to help your hurts."

Josie walked along talking. She dug sassafras roots and picked the branches off the wild cherry trees. By the time they got to

Josie's cabin, Laura had learned that powdered slippery elm bark, mixed with mineral water, heals a sick stomach, and that every part of the elder plant is used as medicine.

Laura hesitated on entering Josie's cabin. "You want me to wait out on the porch?"

Josie held the crooked old door open. "Come on in, Laura, and sit down."

The inside of the cabin was as strange as Josie. There were bottles and jars on every surface. Roots, branches, and bark hung from the ceiling. In the fireplace, a pot was boiling, which Josie sampled.

"This is just about ready, Laura. Try it," Josie said, putting the spoon to Laura's mouth.

Laura closed her eyes and swallowed. "It's good!" she said, surprised.

"Durn right it's good. Made it myself." Josie smiled.

"What's in it?"

"I call it my good-for-what-ails-you tonic." She ladled some off into a Mason jar and capped it, handing it to Laura. "Take this home."

Laura looked at the root- and branch-filled jar and the amber liquid. Josie pointed around the jar. "That's cherry tree bark; it'll help you if you got a cold, 'cause it'll make you sweat. That's bloodroot to perk you up, make you want to eat. The sassafras gives it flavor, along with the honey."

Laura's head felt clear. It was startling.

"You can feel it already, can't ya?" Josie asked. Then, before Laura could answer, Josie laughed. "Most of the other herb healers put whiskey or grain liquor in their medicines to give it a kick, just like the patent medicines from the stores. I don't take much to drinkin' whiskey, so I just keep mine natural."

Laura waited for the opportunity to bring up the article, but Josie beat her to it. "Laura Wilder, you been wantin' to ask me what I thought about your witches' article and—"

Laura interrupted. "I hadn't planned on it being printed yet—not until I'd come to visit with you."

Josie shook her head. "Don't matter. What you wrote was true. I've read about the witch burnin' at Salem and in Europe. Terrible . . . just terrible."

"You have?"

Josie cackled. "If you had kids callin' you a witch since you were a little girl, then you'd probably get a curious streak too. So I read all the books that I could borrow and know enough about witches to play games back on the kids."

"But Rutherford really believes what he's saying."

Josie shook her head. "I think he's just a crazy man who knows how to use fear to keep his followers in line. Keep people away from other people long enough and they'll believe anything."

A thought came to Laura, so she asked, "Why don't you come to Apple Hill this Saturday? We're throwing our annual get-together."

"Me? You'd want me to come?" Josie asked.

"Why not? It'd give you a chance to meet the people and they could see that you're not a witch."

Josie sighed. "I appreciate what you're tryin' to do, I really do. But I've lived alone for so many years, I just feel comfortable bein' away from folks."

"Will you at least think about it?" Laura asked.

"I'll think about it." Josie smiled. "Now, let me get you some of this tea to take the pain and stiffness out of your husband."

Laura would have been surprised to know that after she left, Josie started crying. *I'm just the old maid of the mountains,* Josie thought. *Never been kissed by a boy. The only hugs I ever got were from my parents. Never danced with a man. Never sat and ate with a man who wanted to be with me. I never had anyone 'cept my folks say "I love you."*

For the first time since her parents died from the fever, Josie began sobbing. *I never wanted to be ugly. Don't they know that it hurts real bad when they call me a witch?*

It all came back to her in a flood. The school taunts. The jeering children. Boys throwing rocks at her when she went to town.

Oh, Momma, she sighed, *you were so kind to me, keepin' me away from all the meanness. Is that why we lived way out here, away from people?*

Josie looked in the small, cracked mirror that hung on her wall. She thought of her father, hugging her in front of this same mirror, telling her that God loves all His children.

"Josie," he told her, "you are what you are. You ain't never gonna be the belle of the ball, but your ma and I love you just the way God made you. You understand me, girl?"

Josie had nodded, wiping back the tears. Now she looked into that same mirror and wished her father was there. *I miss you, Pa. I do. You made me feel so pretty . . . so special. To you, I was one in a million, I was smart. I had a special touch in the woods.*

Living alone had kept the world at a distance. Those who came around came on her terms.

I don't want to deal with Rutherford or with the sheriff. I don't want to go to parties or visit with people. I don't want people wincing when they look at me.

God made me but my life's my own. If I'm ugly then I'm ugly. That I can't help. But I can help havin' people around, disturbin' me.

CHAPTER 24

TALKIN' TO JUDGMENT

No one was around the barn when Susan came back to the camp. Brother Robert walked up and took her arm. "Rutherford wants you."

"For what?" Susan struggled.

"I don't question his commands," he said.

"Leave me alone," she said loudly.

Brother Robert ignored her cries and pulled her along. Susan resisted, but he just tightened his grip on her arm.

Inside, Rutherford was shuffling a deck of gypsy cards he'd taken from a fortune teller's tent on their way to Missouri. When he saw the gypsy's tent, Rutherford had a vision of fire—flames leaping, engulfing the earth. So he and Brother Robert returned later and torched the tent, destroying all the gypsy's evil tools. The only thing they saved were her cards, which Rutherford now used to walk the line he saw between good and evil in the world.

He shuffled the cards and arranged them into a pattern similar to what he saw the gypsy do. The cards fascinated him. It was like touching evil over the centuries, taking him back to the great witch burnings two hundred years before.

He looked for signs in the cards before him. *This one means the future is now,* he thought, *and this one tells me I need strength.* He nodded, picking up the colorful card. *And this one means I will be fighting a witch and this one* . . . He looked at the card at the bottom of the pattern. *This one means someone is going to die.*

Rutherford closed his eyes, praying to himself, trying to understand the cards—repulsed by his even having them, much less laying them out.

"The cards are evil!" he screamed, slamming his fist down, sending dust dancing through the stuffy air. Behind him he heard the barn door being unlatched.

Brother Robert shoved Susan ahead of him as they came inside. Rutherford was sitting on the snake's crate. He scooped the cards up and put them into his pocket as Brother Robert latched the barn door.

"Be quiet," he whispered to Susan. "Judgment's asleep."

"Let me go. I want to go home," she whispered.

"Shhh," Rutherford said, putting his finger to his lips, "he doesn't like to be awakened."

Susan nodded, then was dumbstruck when Rutherford hit the side of the crate with his staff. "Stop. Stop it," she whispered.

Rutherford whacked the cage again. "Don't get Judgment mad; he hasn't eaten for a while." He opened the crate and turned to Susan. "He likes to eat rats. Did you know that?"

Lifting Judgment out of the box, he put his face up to the snake's head. "Which one of us will have her? You or I, Judgment?"

Susan cringed into the shadows. "Stop this. Stop."

Rutherford closed his eyes as the snake's head darted back and forth around him. "Oh, Judgment, which one of us will have her? Will Susan become my wife or will she become a sign for you? Which shall it be?"

"No . . . no!" Susan cried, trying to open the door.

Rutherford turned. "Did you have a nice chat with that witch's friend?"

"What are you talkin' about?" Susan asked.

Rutherford walked toward her with the snake. "Don't lie to me. I know everything. I saw you in the woods, following that Wilder woman like a shadow." He edged closer, lifting the snake over his head. "What did you tell her?"

Susan struggled with the door. "I didn't tell her anything. I just wanted to know her name and why she was going to see the witch."

Rutherford stopped. "You can't change witches, but witches can change you. Did she touch you?"

"No. No."

Rutherford shook his head. "I think you've forgotten the way." He turned to Brother Robert. "Don't you think she's backslid? Don't you think she's not in the path with the Flock?"

Brother Robert nodded. "She needs to be cleansed."

"Later, the cleansing can wait." He walked close enough so that the snake could reach her, but the snake just hissed his tongue in and out.

Rutherford smiled. "Signs are that you are telling the truth. Which answers the question I asked Judgment." He looked at Susan. "You will be mine. You will be my wife. I have seen it in a vision."

Resting the snake on his shoulders, he chuckled. "Our marriage will be until death do us part. Do you understand?"

Susan slipped down against the door, crying.

CHAPTER 25

HOME REMEDIES

Sheriff Peterson was waiting at Apple Hill Farm when Laura returned.

Laura waved. "Sheriff, what brings you here?"

Peterson shook his head. "Sorry to be comin' up here on official business, but I'm tryin' to make sense out of this whole mess."

They sat on the front porch. Peterson took off his hat and sighed. "I been over talkin' to that Rutherford man and up to see Josie. He calls her a witch and she calls him crazy. What do you think?"

Laura lifted her hair off her neck. "I think that what happened to that dead man has nothin' to do with Josie and everything to do with that man and his Flock."

"What do you mean?"

Laura told him about meeting Susan Ponder and their strange conversation. "What do you think she meant by snake cleansing?" Peterson asked.

Laura closed her eyes for a moment. "I think that her husband wasn't bit in the woods. I think he died in the barn, doin' whatever Rutherford makes them do with that big snake."

Peterson shivered. "Just thinkin' about snakes gives me the willies. I can't imagine handling one for fun."

Laura looked him in the eye. "Sheriff, I think something bad's going on at the old Williams place. I think someone else is going to get snake bit."

"I don't know what I can do about it." He shrugged. "People in this country are free to pray the way they want. Heck, if they wanted to pray to raccoons playin' the banjo on Sunday at high noon, there ain't a durn thing I could do about it."

"Praying and killing are different, Sheriff," Laura said. "One's good and one's evil. There's a difference and you know it."

"What can I do? Rutherford says that the man got snake bit out on a walk. Says that Josie's a witch and she cursed him or somethin'. Josie says that Rutherford is strange and his Flock handles snakes. Rutherford says that's just witch's talk."

Peterson shook his head. "Witches, snakes, dead bodies—this is enough to make me go back to bein' a farmer."

"It's too late to say that. But I don't know what you can do about it," Laura said.

Peterson stood up and tipped his hat. "I just stopped by to chat. I got to get goin'."

"You're coming to the party we're having here Saturday, aren't you?"

"The first party I ever came to in America was here at Apple Hill. You know I wouldn't miss it."

Laura went up to her thinking rock to reflect on things. She wanted to write an article about Josie and her herb medicine, but had trouble thinking about it. Thoughts of Susan Ponder hiding behind the tree, afraid of Rutherford, kept coming to mind.

Manly brought the cows in and came up the ridge. "Laura, you goin' to sit up there all night?"

Laura turned and noticed that he was limping worse than usual. "What's wrong with your leg?"

Manly shook his head. "My back and leg's been actin' up on me again. Think I might need to take my Saturday night bath tonight."

Laura stood up and took Manly's hand. "I got something back in the house I want you to try."

"What is it?" Manly asked suspiciously as they walked along.

"Oh, just a little tonic that Josie made up for you."

Manly stopped and squeezed her hand. "Unh-uh, no, no. I ain't takin' nothin' that she sent."

Laura pulled him along. "Why? I spent a lot of time with her in the woods and—"

"I think you must have spent too much time in the sun."

"Oh, Manly, she knows what she's talking about. Why, she's an expert on roots and herbs."

Manly snorted. "I don't care if she's Mother Nature herself. I'm not takin' any backwoods whatever."

In the kitchen, Laura showed him the root- and leaf-filled jar. Manly shook his head. "Looks like the scrapin's off a dustpan."

Laura opened the lid. "Just a little taste. She said it would help your miseries."

Manly sniffed it. "Whoo-whee. That smells like old shoes! Drinkin' this would make anyone miserable!" He looked Laura in the eye. "If the stuff's so good, why don't you take some first?"

Laura hadn't expected this and had to think fast. She wanted Manly to be the guinea pig. "Because I don't have a sore back. All that's aching on me is my tummy."

"Why didn't you have her make somethin' up for you?"

Without thinking, Laura exclaimed, "Why, she did make me up a jar of what she called good-for-what-ails-you tonic." She opened the pantry and reached in. "Here it is."

Manly looked at her root-filled jar. "Go ahead, drink some."

Laura opened the jar, closed her eyes, and touched her tongue to the brown liquid. *It didn't taste bad!*

"How's it taste?" Manly asked, smiling devilishly.

"Pretty good," she smiled.

Before she could get him to try his, he held out a coffee cup. "Pour some of that in here and drink it down. It's good for whatever the heck ails you," he smiled.

Laura took the dare and poured a half cup. She took a sip and stuck her tongue out at Manly. "Scaredy cat."

Manly laughed and Laura drank some more. It cleared her nostrils, opened her throat, and sent a jolt through her system. "Maybe this will help me out," she said, already feeling refreshed.

She looked at Manly. "Now you try some."

He slowly opened his jar and touched his tongue in it. "It tastes like a dead squirrel was soaked in this water!"

"It can't taste that bad," she laughed.

"Worse," he said, peering into the jar. "I think the squirrel's inside it someplace."

Later that evening, sitting at her desk, Laura began another article.

Old-Fashioned Health Remedies Work!
By Laura Ingalls Wilder

Did you know that nature has a fruit, herb, or vegetable that has an ingredient for almost every internal weakness that affects us? Do you know that just outside your door is a wonderful, natural pharmacy?

Now, I believe in going to doctors and am not advocating anyone rushing out into the woods and eating whatever they find. But I am saying that I was impressed by my visit to Josie Tatum, the herb woman of the mountains, and am going to try to learn more.

Like Mother Nature, she's standing on the ridge above town, with her hands on her hips, calling us to come back to the old-fashioned health remedies that worked.

Your parents and grandparents had the wisdom of the ages, which we seem to be losing to our love of patent medicines. Isn't it funny that even though we are building more hospitals and inventing more medicines, all of mankind seems on the verge of a health crisis?

Josie told me that herbs have been with us since the beginning of time; that we've used herbs to treat illnesses throughout all recorded history. Though she's not an openly religious woman, she showed me in the Bible where God tells us to use herbs to benefit our health.

The Egyptians were skilled herbalists, and written texts on papyrus reveal over 700 herbal remedies. The Chinese have healed with herbs for over 5,000 years. Hippocrates, the Greek "father of medical literature," believed and taught that in nature there is strength to cure disease. He used diet and herbs as the basis of treatment.

Josie Tatum may look strange to some of you, but her wisdom of the woods is strictly common sense. Is using herbs, fruits, and vegetables to cure what ails you superstitious? Not on your life! Making your life better through natural means is what Josie is preaching.

Here are just a few of the herbal old-fashioned remedies that she taught me.

When Laura finished the article, describing all the leaves, roots, and stems that Josie had shown her, she put her pencil down. *It's a good story, one that should end the witchcraft talk,* Laura thought. She phoned the story into Summers and called it a day, quite satisfied with herself.

At Mom's Cafe the next morning, Mom picked up the paper and read Laura's article to Hambone. "That woman moves quick," Mom said.

Hambone looked puzzled. "I don't know what you mean?"

Mom hugged him. "Oh, Hambone, what I mean is just a few days ago, the whole town was abuzz over her witchcraft article, and now we'll all be talkin' 'bout eatin' things from the woods."

"Hope it won't be bad for business," Hambone said.

Mom laughed. "People talk about growin' their own food and eatin' right, but they're just downright lazy. That's why there's fewer farmers each year and more restaurants. No one wants to grow food, but they all sure want to eat it—especially when someone else's cookin' it!"

"Maybe someone besides Hambone," Otis said sarcastically. "This soup is awful! Almost makes you wanna move away."

Hambone glared. "If you don't like it, don't eat here."

Otis laughed. "I'm just kiddin', Hambone."

Mom walked over and stood at the counter. "What would make you move?"

Otis shrugged. "Some of the conjurers up in the hills have this formula to make someone move away."

"What is it?" Hambone laughed. "Let a skunk loose in their house?"

Otis smiled. "I hear that they take some hair off a dead cat, fill its mouth with new potatoes covered with red wax, then wrap the cat in a white paper."

"That's it?" Mom asked.

"Let me finish," Otis said. "Then you tell the dead cat what you want to happen and place it under the house of the person you want to move away."

Mom threw her hands up and walked away. "How can folks believe such craziness? Must be a full moon every night over the Ozarks!"

Hambone went back to his cooking. "Like I said, dead cat and stinkin' skunk—they'll both smell up your house."

Outside of town, Rutherford finished reading Laura's article on Josie and ripped the paper to shreds. "This is witch's trickery!" he cried out to the hills. "Laura Ingalls Wilder is trying to make that witch seem human!"

In a fit of rage, his face turned purple and his eyes bulged out. He turned to Brother Robert. "If she wants to defend witches, then let her be known as a witch. Tonight I want you to put a sign for all to know." He handed Brother Robert a gypsy card—the card of impending death.

"This is the sign I see. This is what I see for those who defend witches," he said, then turned another card. "And this is the sign I see for the witch," he said, showing Brother Robert the second card.

"Is this what you see in your vision?" Brother Robert asked.

"I feel the call for Judgment coming," Rutherford said.

CHAPTER 26

SATURDAY NIGHT BATH ON FRIDAY

Terry was convinced he had been hexed. He'd heard Josie say the word *curse,* thought she'd said "cursed," and just figured that she'd hexed him.

"What am I going to do?" he asked Larry, walking out toward the school play area to eat lunch.

"Let's talk about it while we eat."

"You really gonna take Mr. Springer up on his dare?" Terry asked.

"We all are, 'cause we're the Younguns."

Terry thought about walking through the graveyard and going into that old house. "Might have to change my last name," he mumbled.

"What was that?" Larry asked.

"Nothin'. Just my stomach grumblin'."

They found their lunch sacks and headed for the shade tree behind the school, where they always sat. Terry kept lifting his bag up and down.

"Mine feels a lot lighter than this morning," he said, frowning.

Larry shrugged. "Did you eat anythin' while you were walking?"

"Nope," Terry said. He opened his sack. "Hey! My pie's gone!"

Larry opened his sack. "Mine, too!"

From around the play area, other kids were finding their desserts gone. A couple of the Hardacre boys started pointing to Terry. "I didn't do it," he shouted to them. "But I bet I know who did," he said under his breath.

"Who?" Larry asked.

"Come on, let's see," Terry said, heading toward the outhouse.

As they got closer, Terry whispered, "I bet Sweet is hidin' in there."

The door was latched, so Terry shouted, "I need to go bad!"

Sweet answered back, "Wait your turn."

The privy had been secured to the ground so the kids couldn't tip it over as a prank. A four-by-four post was planted five feet in the ground with the privy nailed firmly to it.

Terry winked at Larry and sneaked around the back. He wiggled out a knothole, like he'd done it before, and shouted in, "Hey Sweet Tooth, would you move to the other hole, we're tryin' to finish paintin' under this seat!"

Sweet could be heard trying to move and moaning. "All right, but this is a heck of a time to be paintin'."

Terry knocked again. "Come out, come out, whoever you are."

Sweet answered back, "Terry, you know darn well it's me."

"Me who?" Terry giggled.

"Me Sweet."

"Oh, I thought it was the pie thief."

"What are you talkin' about?" Sweet asked.

"You know durn well, and you better 'fess up fast."

Sweet pulled his pants up and peeked his head out. He had a multicolored pie and cake ring around his mouth. "I don't know what you're talkin' about."

Larry laughed. "Sweet, you got enough evidence 'round your lips to start a bakery."

Sweet licked a circle around his lips. "Does anyone else know?"

"Why'd you do it?" Terry asked.

Sweet shrugged. "When the teacher put me in the cloakroom for talkin', I got bored. And when I get bored I get hungry, and I only had two doughnuts in my pocket so I just began snoopin' and—"

Terry shook his head. "And you ate everyone's dessert, including mine."

"Sorry," Sweet said, hanging his head.

"You owe me, Sweet, you owe me," Terry said, walking off.

"Me too!" said Larry.

"Come on by my dad's bakery this afternoon and I'll sneak you out some doughnuts."

As they walked away, Terry remembered what he wanted to talk about. "What about my hex? How am I goin' to get it off?" He closed one eye and thought for a moment. "Let's go to the library after school and look it up."

When the bell rang, they headed to town, but had one stop to make before the library. The Younguns waited behind the bakery and, true to his word, Sweet sneaked out a dozen doughnuts. They hadn't told who the pie thief was, and after Sweet washed his face, he denied all wrongdoing, even exclaiming that someone had eaten his pie, too!

Sherry ate her sugar-coated doughnut in one bite and reached for another. "Slow down there, tapeworm," Larry said, holding the box high. "We got to make these last."

The boys left Sherry to sit with two doughnuts outside the library, and they went inside to look.

"How do you spell hex?" Larry asked.

Terry shrugged. "X?"

"X! That's not the way. I think it's Hx."

It took them a while to figure out how to spell it because they didn't want to ask the librarian. She sang in the choir at their father's church and would surely wonder why the minister's sons were interested in such things.

Larry pulled out several books. The first one he opened scared him, so he closed the cover and looked around. It was the dictionary.

"Did it say what she done to me?" Terry whispered.

Larry nodded. "Listen to this. The dictionary says that a hex is an 'evil spell or a curse. To wish or bring bad luck to a person through superstitious means.' "

"Oh, no," Terry moaned. "What else does it say?"

"That's all, but let's look in this one," Larry said, pulling out a book that had cost the library twenty-five cents.

HERMANN'S
WIZARDS' MANUAL
Contains Secrets of
Magic, Spirits, Mind Reading,
and Ventriloquism

"What's it say?" Terry whispered.

Larry pulled him along behind the stacks of books until they were hidden in the corner. "It says, 'This book is a complete compendium of the secrets. It tells how to be a spirit medium and the rules to observe when forming spiritual circles.' "

Terry stopped him. "I'm hexed, not circled."

"Let's try this one," he said, opening a ten-cent book.

The Great Books of
Wonders, Secrets, and Mysteries

"Listen to this," Larry said. " 'This book is filled with strange secrets, wonderful mysteries, and startling disclosures. All about Witches and Witchcraft and—' "

Terry stopped him. "Read about witches. Hurry!"

Larry read the information to a wide-eyed Terry. All Terry could do was moan and moan some more.

Larry read on. " 'The dark night of superstition will never end, and no day will ever break to eliminate the well-placed hex without asking the spirits for help.' "

Terry gripped Larry's arm. "Where do I find spirits?"

"I don't know."

Terry was perplexed. "What's a spirit?"

"Let's see," Larry said, opening the dictionary back up. "It says here that . . ." Larry shook his head.

"What's it say?" Terry asked.

"Don't make sense. It talks about 'the spirit of 1776.' "

"Where do I find this 1776 spirit?"

"Maybe that's an address," Larry said, as he continued reading. "Listen to this. 'Spirits are an alcohol solution or alcoholic beverage.' "

Terry looked at him. "You mean like at Tippy's Saloon? Why would a witch be puttin' a drunk's curse on me?"

Larry shrugged. "I don't think this is helpin' us much. Maybe you should just go back to that witch and ask her to uncurse you."

"And what if she curses me again? Then I'm double-cursed."

"Hadn't thought of that." Larry shrugged.

Outside the library, they found Sherry asleep in the sun. Larry had to piggyback her home.

When they got home, they found their father in a tizzy. "What's up, Pa?" Larry asked.

"You kids are late. Where've you been?"

"We were at the library, studyin'," Terry said, smiling.

Rev. Youngun looked down at Terry's shoes. "I thought you went back to get your new shoes."

"We found Larry's and Sherry's, but we couldn't find mine," Terry said. "Maybe some old man found 'em and walked off in 'em."

"An old man? Why would you say that?" his father asked.

"Just a thought."

"Well, I think you ought to go look again tomorrow. Shoes are too expensive to just lose like that."

"Yes, Pa," Terry said.

Rev. Youngun clapped his hands. "I want you all to go up now and take a bath. Terry's first, Sherry's second, and Larry's third."

Larry didn't like the order. "Might as well not even take a bath bein' third. I'll just be sittin' in dirty water."

Rev. Youngun nodded. "If it's too soapy, then draw some extra water to rinse off with."

"Why do we got to take a Saturday night bath on Friday?" Terry asked his father.

"I told you, Carla Pobst is coming to dinner and we're going to the Apple Hill party tomorrow, so we won't have time before Sunday service."

"Why not just skip it?" Terry asked.

"Yea," Larry said, "waitin' a week won't hurt us."

"They'll be holdin' their noses in church around you if you don't. I don't want people callin' my children the three little stinkers."

"We could just put a lot of your smelly water on, Pa," Terry said.

Rev. Youngun looked at his watch. "I got to go."

"How long you gonna be gone, Pa?" Sherry asked.

Rev. Youngun looked at his watch as he tousled her hair. "I'll be back in an hour if Carla's train is on time."

The Younguns reluctantly went upstairs to start the bathwater. In early America, bathing was difficult, and washing your neck, face, arms, and feet just once a week was considered adequate.

Terry knew all about the history of bathing. He listened to a bathtub salesman's pitch once and had memorized it enough to repeat the same things at every bath time.

Standing at the top of the stairs, Terry called out, "I don't want to take a bath. Queen Elizabeth only took one a month."

"Take a bath, Terry," his father answered back. "Cleanliness is next to godliness."

"Nothin' wrong with dirt. Who made the earth?"

"God."

"Right, so He made dirt also. So I'm just keepin' a little godly dirt on me, that's all."

"In the bath, young man."

Terry pouted and started down the stairs. "Boston was right

when they made it unlawful to take a bath 'cept for doctor's orders."

Rev. Youngun sighed. "That was years ago. Now *I'm* orderin' you to take a bath."

As Terry went back up the stairs, he said over his shoulder, "They didn't even put a bathtub in the White House until 1850."

"But they have one now, so go sit in the bath like the president does."

Terry walked into his room, grumbling. "Why don't you take a bath? I didn't ask this lady to dinner, you did."

"Don't disappear on me," Rev. Youngun called back as he headed out the door. "I want everyone in their Sunday best when Carla gets here."

"Do I gotta?"

"Take a bath, Terry," his father shouted once more, as he guided the buggy onto the road.

Terry looked at the tub and shook his head. *No sense wastin' water,* he thought, so he stepped in and stepped out. Then he stuck his fingers in the water, wiggled them around, and cleaned his ears. Finishing, he shouted out, "Sherry, your turn."

Sherry stuck her head in. "It's time for you to disappear. I don't want you seein' me naked."

That gave Terry an idea. He sneaked back into his room, looked under the bed, and pulled out the jar of disappearing cream.

"Maybe this will keep that woman from tryin' to be our ma," Terry said, nodding his head. Then he had another thought. "Sherry, I got somethin' for you."

"What?" she asked from the bath.

"Some fancy French cream that I bought for you at the general store."

"You bought me a present?" she asked suspiciously.

"Yup. I just wanted to make up to you for all the things I done."

"Why now?" she asked, doubting him.

"Well, like what if you disappeared or somethin'. I'd want your last thought to be that I did somethin' nice for you."

"Slip it behind the door."

"Nope. Put a towel on and come out. I want to hand it to you."

"All right," she grumbled. "But you better not be trickin' me."

Sherry got out of the bath and wrapped herself in a towel. Poking her head around the door frame, she began blinking. "Hurry, I got soap in my eyes. I can't see."

Terry couldn't believe his good luck. He quickly opened the jar and took a glob of the cream. "Here it is," he said, globbing it into her hand. "See you later."

"Where you goin'?" she asked, rubbing the sticky cream around in her hand.

"It's where *you're goin'*," he said, smiling.

Larry came out of his room. "Is it my turn yet?" He stopped when he saw what Terry was doing. "Sherry, wash your hands, quick!"

"What . . . why?" she said, blinking.

"Terry put disappearin' cream in your hand."

Sherry screamed and ran back into the bath. Larry took Terry by the shoulders. "That was dumb."

Terry shrugged. "Dumb was tellin' her to wash it off. A moment later and she'd been a goner."

"That stuff ain't real anyway."

"Wanna bet?" Terry said. "Put some on your face, smarty pants!"

Larry reached out, then pulled his hand back. "This is silly. If it was really disappearin' cream, then why didn't you disappear when you touched it?"

Terry thought for a moment, then said, "Disappearin' cream don't make the person rubbin' it on someone else disappear. That's a fact."

"Where'd you learn that?" Larry asked.

"I read a disappearin' book about it."

"You read a book. Where is it?"

"Book just disappeared after I read it. Darndest thing I've ever seen."

Larry whispered, "I got a little plan to keep this woman from liking Pa. This is it . . ."

An hour later, the three Younguns were lined up like angels as Carla arrived. Rev. Youngun helped her from the buggy, then took her arm as he escorted her up the stairs.

Carla smiled. "Larry, Terry, Sherry. It's good to see you again."

Larry nodded. "Good to see you, Mrs. Pobst."

Sherry smiled. "Hi."

Rev. Youngun was relieved, but when Terry didn't say something right away, he cleared his throat.

"Ah, Terry, say hello to Mrs. Pobst."

"Hello, it's a pleasure to see you again," he said, shaking her hand, which was very out of character.

Carla was impressed. "My, you are such a little gentleman. Your father has taught you well."

Terry nodded. "Manners and cleanliness are next to godliness," he said, smiling.

Rev. Youngun saw the glint in Terry's eye and knew something was up. "Ah, children, let's go inside. Please sit with Mrs. Pobst while I check on dinner."

Alone in the parlor, Carla smiled at the three children who were staring at her. "Is there anything wrong?"

The children just stared.

"Is there anything you'd like to ask me?"

Sherry piped up. "Why are you here?"

Carla was caught off guard. "Why, I came to visit with your father and—"

Larry jumped in. "Where are you stayin'? Here?"

"Oh heavens, no," Carla laughed. "I'm staying at the Mansfield Hotel."

Sherry gave her the once-over. "Why do they call you Mrs. Pobst if you ain't married no more?"

"Well," Carla paused, "that's just the custom when your spouse dies and—"

"Is it a custom to want to marry a minister widower?" Larry asked.

Before she could answer, Terry asked, "Why do you want to marry our pa?"

"We're just good friends," Carla said.

Larry asked. "But you went buggy ridin', didn't you?"

"But that doesn't mean we're getting married," she said.

"You ever talk 'bout gettin' married?" Sherry asked.

Carla looked between them, wishing she could switch the topic. "Oh, we've talked about it, but that's all for now. Let's talk about something else. How have you children been feeling?"

Larry shook his head. "Not as bad as Pa."

"Is there something wrong with your father?"

This was the scheme the Younguns had worked out. They had concocted a plan to drive her away.

"Pa's ticker's 'bout ready to give out," Terry said.

"It is?" Carla asked, very concerned.

"You don't want to marry an old man, do you?" Sherry asked.

"Well, he's not old. He's only forty," Carla said.

"He'll be forty-two this summer," Larry said.

"I didn't know that," Carla said, smiling. She'd figured out what the kids were up to.

"And he's got false teef," Sherry said.

"My goodness."

"And he wears a two-play," Terry added.

"He means toupee," Larry said. "Yup, old Pa is a regular bald eagle under that rug."

"I didn't know," Carla said.

"And his eyebrows are glued on," Sherry said, nodding.

"Goodness gracious," Carla sighed. She expected some resistance to her seeing their father, but this came out of the blue. "Does your father know you're telling me all this?"

Six eyes went wide. The kids looked at each other. Larry spoke up. "No, he wouldn't want us tellin' you 'bout his problems, since he likes you. But he's got his burial plot all picked out. We just thought you should know so you could go find another man to marry."

Carla lifted Sherry up onto her lap. "I don't think you children have anything to worry about. Thomas and I are just good friends. Whatever happens will happen. Now why don't you two boys go out to the kitchen and help your father."

"What 'bout me?" Sherry asked.

Carla winked and took a brush out of her purse. "I'm going to brush your hair into braids."

"Braids? Do you know how? Pa doesn't," Sherry said.

"There are some things that men teach boys and some things that women teach girls," Carla said, brushing Sherry's hair.

As the boys walked toward the kitchen, Terry mumbled, "She's got Sherry wrapped around her finger now."

Larry shrugged. "She's not that bad, you know."

"I got a plan," Terry whispered.

"What?"

"Gonna make her disappear for good," he said, pointing to the jar of disappearing cream he'd hidden behind the umbrella stand in the hall.

"You can't do that!" Larry protested.

"Watch me—or I should say, watch *her* disappear," Terry said, chuckling.

Sherry smiled at Carla. "You're nice," she said. "You're not like Terry says you are."

Carla nodded. Thomas Youngun had warned her that his kids weren't happy that he was seeing her, but that it was only natural in the beginning.

"Oh, and what does Terry say?"

"He says that you tricked Pa into buggy ridin' monkey business and that you want to move in and eat all our food."

Carla laughed. "My word, why would he say all that?"

Sherry thought for a moment. "Maybe 'cause he's hexed."

"Hexed?" Carla exclaimed, dropping the brush.

"That's right, hexed. Josie the witch cursed him with a hex and he don't know how to get it off."

By the time Sherry had finished telling all about the shoe tree, the hex, and Old Fred, it was all Carla could do to keep a straight face. "Do you want me to help Terry?" she asked.

Sherry shrugged. "I don't think anyone can help Terry, least that's what Pa says."

"What's that?"

"Pa says that Terry is a born rascal. Can't change what you're born with, can you Miss Carla?"

"I guess not," she smiled, hugging Sherry.

Rev. Youngun walked into the parlor. "Everything's ready."

Carla smiled. "I've never known a man who could cook up a whole meal. I'm impressed, Thomas."

"Can't take all the credit myself," Rev. Youngun said, smiling. "Two church ladies came by and helped get things ready."

"And I heard 'em talkin' 'bout you two gettin' married," Sherry said.

Clearly embarrassed, Rev. Youngun blushed. "Sherry, that's not somethin' to be talkin' about."

"Sorry, Pa."

Carla hugged her. "That's okay. I kind of like talking about it."

Sherry jumped off her lap and ran toward the kitchen. "Let's eat."

Carla stood up and took Rev. Youngun's hand. "One out of three, Thomas. I think she likes me."

"How could anyone *not* like you."

At the table, Terry waited for his chance. Every time his father left to get something from the kitchen, he'd stick his fingers in the jar hidden in his lap. But each time, just as he was about to put the disappearing cream on Carla, his father would come back in.

Finally, he saw his chance when Sherry and Larry helped carry the plates to the kitchen. He grabbed Carla's hand and began rubbing the cream on. "We always rub this homemade health cream on our hands after dinner."

"You do?" Carla asked, caught off guard.

Terry rubbed it all over her hands. "Yup, kind of a family tradition."

Carla pinched her nose at the smell. "This smells like wintergreen rubbing ointment."

"I think it is."

"Why are you rubbing so hard?" Carla asked.

"Supposed to rub it in until it disappears," Terry smiled.

Sherry came back in and saw the jar in Terry's lap. "Stop, stop!" she screamed out.

"What? What's wrong?" Carla asked.

Sherry began crying hysterically. "Don't disappear! Rub it off!" she cried out to Terry.

Rev. Youngun came in. "What's wrong?" Larry stood sheepishly behind him.

Carla shrugged. "Terry wanted to rub some homemade health cream on me; said it was an old after-dinner family tradition."

Rev. Youngun looked at Terry. "What tradition?" In two steps, he was standing beside his son. "And what's in this jar?" he asked, picking it up.

Terry was speechless, but Sherry said, "It's disappearin' cream, Pa."

"Disappearin' cream?" he asked. "Terry, what's goin' on?"

"Terry was just kidding, weren't you, Terry?" Carla said, winking at him.

Terry coughed, unable to believe his own good luck. "Certainly, Pa. I was just pullin' a trick and—"

"And he needs to have a hex removed, Thomas," Carla said.

"A hex?" Rev. Youngun exclaimed.

"I think they need to tell you about Josie and the shoe tree and how it all started."

Rev. Youngun took off his apron. "Let's go into the parlor and talk about it."

Terry looked at Carla as they left the room. "Thanks . . . pal."

"Don't mention it . . . pal." Carla winked and tousled his hair.

In the parlor, Rev. Youngun listened to Larry explain what had happened, but couldn't help noticing Terry snuggled against Carla on the sofa. *Two down, one to go,* he thought.

After the incredible tale was finished, he took their hands and looked into their eyes. "There's no such thing as witches or ghosts and let me tell you why."

Even though the children listened with rapt attention, each of them was thinking about Friday the 13th coming up and Old Fred. Sometimes common sense and superstition are miles apart in a child's mind—especially when you've been dared.

CHAPTER 27

A SIGN

Later that evening, Manly was sure he heard something on the front porch, but he saw nothing from the window.

"Probably just the wind," Laura said from under the covers.

Sliding back under the sheets, Manly shrugged. "Sounded like someone walkin' 'round out there."

"Get some sleep. We've got a lot of people coming over tomorrow."

Laura drifted off quickly, but for the rest of the night, Manly had a fitful sleep. He knew he'd heard something.

Across the ridge, Rutherford held up his hand to block the moonlight from his face. Everything was confusing.

He didn't like being out after dark, yet he found himself out in the very evil darkness he preached against. He railed against signs of evil and witches' tools, but was using gypsy cards to look for signs.

Were the books he'd read about witches, or the witches' market back in Georgia, confusing his mind? Was he losing track of his mission and entering the realm of the shadowy sisterhood?

The moon was full and the stars sparkled in the darkness. He raised his staff to the night and spoke to the heavens. "Wizards once gazed at the stars to understand the past and what was to come. The stars give sailors direction, yet evil men study the constellations to divine the future. They believe that planets govern the human body and all creation."

In his heart he believed that studying the stars for signs was wrong, silly, and inherently evil. Yet he couldn't stop searching the heavens for the planet with the sign.

Cupping his fingers into a primitive telescope, he narrowed his focus and spotted it—Saturn, the planet he knew stood for disorder and chaos. He waited for the vision to come, but nothing came.

"Where is the vision?" Rutherford screamed into the night. He turned at the sound behind him. It was Brother Robert.

"Did you leave the message?" Rutherford asked him.

"I did as you ordered," the burly man said.

"Let us get out of the dark then," Rutherford said, turning around.

As usual, Laura awoke first and lay in the bed, waiting for her body to greet the day. She thought about Josie complaining about all the kids running around, preparing for the race.

It ain't good for them, she'd said. *Did your grandma ever do sit-ups or run around like Indians were chasing her? Did she ever lift dumbbells, which are pretty well named if you ask me.*

Laura thought about Josie's doses of common sense. She thought about how a dog stretches out and yawns, then stretches again as it gets up from sleeping. So she stretched her legs, then her arms, wiggling her fingers and toes.

Remembering how her mother used to wake up, Laura sat on the side of the bed and stretched her arms. Then she stood up and bent back with her hands on her hips. *It does feel good,* she thought, yawning again.

Laura was looking out through the curtains when Manly finally woke up. He groaned, roared, wheezed, coughed, blew his nose, and made enough other sounds to scare an army away.

"You must be feeling pretty good to make all that racket," she said.

"Didn't sleep hardly a wink. I swore I heard someone out creepin' around last night."

Manly did a quick check of the livestock, then sat in the kitchen for his morning cup of coffee. Laura checked the windows, then walked out on the front porch and screamed.

Manly rushed out onto the front porch. "What's wrong?"

"Who would have done this?" Laura asked, pointing to the blood-red pentagram painted on the front door. "This is a witch's sign."

Manly was furious. "Some coward who don't like your article."

Laura bent down and picked up the card on the doormat.

"What is it?" Manly asked.

"I think it's a gypsy card," she said, frowning.

"A what?" Manly asked.

"A gypsy card, a fortune-telling card." She looked at the card in her hand and shivered. "There's a dead person on this one."

Manly took the card from her hand. "Someone's playin' a game with us, and I don't like it."

Laura looked out over Apple Hill. "This is Rutherford's doings."

Manly put his arm around her. "I don't like anyone scarin' my wife. I think I'll go and have a talk with him."

Laura couldn't stop him and watched helplessly as Manly rode off on his horse, over the ridge. She occupied herself scrubbing the red sign off her door—trying to scrub it out of her mind at the same time.

Josie awoke to find her own message. Someone had trampled her herb gardens and pulled up the plants. "Who in tarnation would have done this?" she asked out loud, picking up the card left on the smashed planter.

"A gypsy card?" she gasped, looking at the tormented figure.

"That will be your fate!" a voice cried out, echoing over the ravine.

Josie looked around. "Who said that?"

"You and that other witch have been warned!"

Then she saw him. Rutherford was on the top of the ridge, dressed in black, holding the staff above his head.

"You're evil, Rutherford!" she shouted out. "You're the devil's kin!"

Rutherford turned and walked back to the Flock. As he made his way along the trail of bent twigs and piled rocks, he thought, *That will teach the witch. I destroyed her poison garden.*

He thought about the plants. In his mind her herb garden was filled with nightshade, hemlock, and yew—all plants of death.

He was so involved in his thoughts that he bumped headlong into Manly's horse. "What are you doin' on our property?" he demanded.

Manly looked him in the eye. "I want to know what you were doin' on ours?"

Rutherford tried to walk around, but Manly maneuvered the horse to block him. "Let me pass," Rutherford said.

Manly spat. "I asked you what you were doin' on our property last night."

Rutherford lifted his staff. "I don't know what you're talkin' 'bout."

Manly took out the gypsy card and flipped it into Rutherford's face. "You left this after you painted up our door."

"I haven't set foot on your land," he said, raising his staff again to protect himself.

Manly kicked the staff away. "If I ever catch you scarin' my wife again, I'll drive you back to Georgia."

"You're crazy," Rutherford said, sneering.

"I ain't the crazy one, but if you or any of your people come sneakin' 'round our place again, I might just go crazy. You know what I'm talkin' 'bout?"

CHAPTER 28

APPLE HILL GET-TOGETHER

Laura spent the morning preparing for their annual get-to-gether, but she was worried. Something was in the air. She could feel it.

Manly didn't say much after he returned, only that he had had words with Rutherford and hoped it was all over. But Laura knew it wasn't.

Manly saw the worry lines on her face and rubbed her shoulders. "Worryin' will kill you, girl. You can't change what's happened and you can't predict what will come. So just close your eyes and accept things, and our lives will be fine."

Laura smiled. Manly's relaxed attitude about life seemed to always keep him in a better mood than she. He did everything at a slower pace and just seemed to worry less.

Manly got the cows out to pasture while Laura checked the ovens. Ladies from her reading club and from the church were expected over at noon, bringing plates of potluck.

"Anybody home?"

Laura put her spoon down and turned. "Josie? What are you doin' here?"

Josie opened the screen door and held out a basket. "Just brought you a few things for your party."

Laura smiled. "You shouldn't have brought all this," she said, looking at the basket filled with mint, flowers, and small berries.

Josie shook her head. "That man Rutherford came 'round and knocked down most of my herb garden. Didn't want it to go to waste."

"You saw him do it?"

"I saw him on the ridge, holdin' up his staff like he was Moses. It was him all right."

"He was here too," Laura said, and she told Josie about the painted sign and the gypsy card.

Josie reached into her pocket. "He left me this," she said, holding out another gypsy card.

"What does it mean?" Laura asked.

"I think it means my life is hanging between life and death."

"Do you think he believes in all this?" Laura asked, fingering the colorful card.

"That fool man talks about fightin' evil, yet he's leavin' callin' cards like this. It don't make sense."

"Do you want me to call the sheriff?" Laura asked.

Josie shook her head. "No, I've got to handle this myself," she said, putting the basket down. "Use the mint for your tea, and the berries in your salad, and—"

"Aren't you coming?"

Josie shook her head. "It's been so long since I've been around people that I wouldn't know what to say."

"But you need to come."

Josie held up her hand. "I haven't bought a dress for thirty years. Been makin' my own and patchin' those. No, people would just stare and whisper about the ugly old lady if I came."

Laura took her arm. "Please come."

Josie sighed. "Laura Ingalls Wilder, you're a good woman. I thank you for invitin' me; it's the nicest thing that anyone's ever done."

"Then you'll come?" Laura asked hopefully.

"No, it's best I be goin'," Josie said, lowering her head and turning to go without another word.

Laura thought she saw a tear in Josie's eye. "Josie, please stay and talk. I'll heat up some coffee and—"

Josie shook her head, sobbing silently, and slipped from Laura's grasp. At the door she stopped and turned, her eyes glistening. "Be careful of Rutherford. He thinks we're *both* witches now."

Josie was up the trail before Laura could call after her.

By early afternoon, the Apple Hill party had started. Laura and Manly had invited over fifty people from the town. Tables were all around the yard, loaded with food.

Laura hadn't told anyone about the sign painted on their door, not even the sheriff. This was an afternoon of fun, and Laura wanted everyone to enjoy themselves.

Hambone came with Mom, Sarah and William Bentley came to talk about the race, and Dr. George and Polly rode over with Maurice and Eulla Mae Springer.

Rev. Youngun brought the widow Pobst with him, and his three children were dressed like they were going to church. Laura had to turn her face to keep from laughing at Terry Youngun. *There's no way that collar button's going to stay buttoned,* she thought, giggling to herself.

Moments later, when his father wasn't looking, Terry just popped the button off and threw it away. "It was squashing my Adam's apple," Terry told his father.

When Rabbi Max Stern, his wife, and son Abe arrived, Laura brightened. "Rabbi Stern, I'm so glad you could come," Laura said, greeting their wagon.

Stern tipped his hat. "I'm just glad you invitationed us. Please let me introduction you to my wife, Tamara," he said nervously, in his broken English.

"You are writer my husband speaks so highly about," Tamara said, looking Laura over.

Laura blushed. "Please, come inside the house."

Abe looked up from the back of the wagon. "We brought you some kosher food," he said, handing over covered plates and pots.

Stern smiled. "This what we do in Russia. Share food with neighbors."

"And you have lots of good neighbors here in Mansfield," Laura said, grinning.

"And so many children," Tamara said.

"They're all ready for the big Founder's Day foot race."

"And when is race?" Rabbi Stern asked.

"Next week, Saturday the fourteenth." Laura watched Abe wave to Terry Youngun and walk over to him. "Is Abe going to be able to enter?"

Tamara Stern shook her head. "I don't think so. He coughing again."

"Maybe a day in the country will make him feel better," Laura said. "Come on, I want to introduce you to everyone."

The get-together was blessed with wonderful weather. Sweet was caught eating a whole pie under the table, but everything else was perfect.

The children climbed the trees, tossed baseballs, and then gathered around Sarah Bentley who, as usual, was dressed in the latest fashion. As the wife of the richest man in the county, she felt she had an image to live up to.

She raised her hands for silence and said to the children, "I just want to make sure that all you children are ready for the foot race next Saturday."

The children cheered and Sarah smiled. Reaching into her purse, she brought out an envelope. "I got this from the bank," she said, taking out a crisp, new ten-dollar bill. "One of you lucky children will get to keep this for winning the race."

The children just stared at the bill. It was more money than any of them had ever had in their lives.

"What will you do with the money?" Sarah asked. "Use it for schoolbooks?"

The kids all looked at each other. Terry Youngun cried out,

"Heck no, buy candy—a lot of candy!" All the kids laughed and jostled Terry around.

"No matter what you do with the money, I just hope that each of you comes out to race. Marathons are the latest rage in Boston and New York, so it'll be good to bring some culture to our little town."

Sarah never quite saw the looks her neighbors gave her, half of them wishing she was back in New York. But Laura had grown to like her, even if she was like a fish out of water.

While Sarah was speaking, no one saw Josie hiding in the woods, peeking at the party. Though she was happy for Laura, she couldn't stop the tears.

Life's not fair! No boy ever asked me to a party. I wanted to get married. I wanted to have children.

Her mind drifted while she watched Rev. Youngun and Carla holding hands. Laura kissing Manly on the cheek. Boys chasing girls. Teenagers making small talk.

The only man who ever kissed me was my father.

Meanwhile, Terry still believed he had a hex, but had forgotten about it for the afternoon. He played hide-and-go-seek with Abe and the other children in the barn. "Did your pa find out that you ate the gumdrops?" he asked Abe, while they hid in the haystack.

"Nope." Abe smiled. "I kept our secret."

Terry tousled Abe's hair and knocked off his yarmulke by mistake. "Sorry," he said, picking it up.

Abe shrugged. "That's okay."

Terry tickled him. "You like wearin' that hat?" Abe couldn't answer because he was laughing so hard. "Cat got your tongue, Abe?"

Abe was laughing so hard that they both rolled out from haystack. Then Abe began coughing, trying to catch his breath.

"You okay, Abe?" Terry asked.

Abe tried to talk but couldn't stop coughing. "Get Father," he managed to whisper.

Terry ran to Rabbi Stern and tugged at his sleeve. "Abe's coughing real bad."

"Where is he?" Stern asked with a worried look on his face.

"He's in the barn. Come on."

They found Abe coughing on his knees, with thick spittle coming out of his throat. His father carried him out into the sunshine and laid him on a blanket.

Several people came running, including Dr. George. "What's wrong with your son?" the doctor asked.

Rabbi Stern shook his head. "He gets coughing fits but this is worst I've seen."

Dr. George sat Abe up and pounded on his back. "His lungs are clogged. You say this has been going on a long time?"

"Since the pox."

"Smallpox?" Dr. George exclaimed. People in the crowd whispered among themselves. Smallpox was a frightening word.

"He had pox in Russia," Stern tried to explain. "But they cured him with cowpox vaccine. There we spent much time in damp root cellars."

Laura knelt down beside Abe, wiping his sweaty forehead with a damp cloth. "He just overdid himself," she said, smiling at Abe. "He'll be all right in a few minutes."

Josie looked down from the ridge. "That boy's sick," she said to herself, heading back to her cabin for coughing tea. "He needs some of my doctorin'."

As she walked quickly through the woods, she thought about what she'd mix together. *Maybe some blue violet and horehound, with a little rosemary and black cohosh. That should stop the coughing. Then I can figure out what's really wrong with the boy.*

Josie walked right past Jackson Rutherford and Brother Robert who had been watching the party from the shadows. Rutherford shook his head. "She reeks of evil, even in daylight."

Brother Robert nodded. "She needs to be cleansed."

"Follow her. I think she's going to get something."

Rutherford watched Brother Robert slip off into the shadows, then turned to watch the panic over the sick boy.

"That boy needs me. Only I can save him," Rutherford whispered to himself. *If I cure him, people will know I have the power. Then they will surely give me all the land I want.*

Down below, Dr. George felt Abe's pulse. "You feelin' dizzy, Abe?"

Abe nodded and his father said, "He sometimes gets dizzy after he coughs. That's why I don't let him run around much."

Suddenly, Abe began coughing again.

"Do you have medicine for him, Doctor?" Stern asked.

Dr. George gently pounded on Abe's back. "First let's stop the coughing, then we'll figure out what he's needin'."

Abe's cough subsided and he put his head against Dr. George's chest. He patted the boy on the head and said, "He needs to rest."

Rabbi Stern sat quietly. "But isn't there anything you can do for my son? He seems to be getting weaker."

"I think you need to bring him into my office on Monday. Let's see what the books say 'bout what's ailin' him."

Terry Youngun tapped Dr. George on the shoulder. "Is my buddy goin' to be all right?"

Abe looked up and smiled. "Hi, Terry," he said weakly.

Rabbi Stern patted Terry on the head. "Maybe you're just what doctor ordered—a friend."

Dr. George picked Abe up and took him into Laura's living room. "Let Abe rest here a while and talk with his friend."

When the rabbi and the doctor were off the porch, Terry reached into his pocket. "Want a gumdrop?" he smiled.

"That is the best medicine of all." Abe smiled, taking the gum drop and popping it into his mouth.

On the other side of the highest ridge, Josie was hurrying along as fast as her old legs would carry her. She'd mixed together the coughing tea with some "get-up-and-run" spirit tea and a bit of her blood-purifying tea.

"This will get him back up," she said to the birds flying by.

She wanted to bring along her red-capped jar of liniment to rub on the boy's chest, but she must have misplaced it. As she moved silently across the shadowed floor of the woods, she hummed a song her mother had taught her.

She was so happy with being able to help that she didn't notice Brother Robert shadowing her with Rutherford right behind him. It had been years since she'd thought of her mother rocking her on the porch, and she sang the words as she remembered them.

". . . how sweet the sound, that saved a wretch like—"

Rutherford was standing behind the tree as she approached. Without warning, he swung his staff and shattered the jar.

Josie was dripping wet, her face covered with bits of herbs and glass, but she didn't blink. "Why'd you do that?" she screamed. "That was herb medicine for the sick boy!"

Rutherford snarled. "You keep away from that boy. He needs to be cleansed, not filled with evil juices."

Josie spat between Rutherford's feet. "You keep your snake away from that boy. You've already killed one person that I know of."

Rutherford's laugh echoed through the ravine. "What are you talkin' about?"

Josie cackled, spinning in circles. "I've seen you talk with that big snake. Oh yes, indeed I have."

Rutherford beat the ground with his staff. "You keep away from the Flock."

Now it was Josie's turn to send laughter echoing through the hills. "You told the sheriff that the man was bit by a snake when he was out walking. He was bit in your barn, bit by that big rattlesnake you call Judgment."

"The spiders have spied for you, haven't they?" Rutherford said. "I crushed one, but there must be more."

Josie shook her head. "Spiders? You're nuttier than a fruitcake, Rutherford. I just looked through the door and saw your crazy goin's on." She pushed him aside. "Now get out of my way."

Rutherford shouted as she walked away, "The boy is mine. Leave him alone!"

At the edge of the clearing around Apple Hill Farm, Josie stood in the shadows of the orchard and whistled to a young boy playing nearby. She didn't know it was Terry.

"Hey boy, come over here."

Terry turned. "What do you want?"

Josie shook her head. "Should have known that the first kid I see would be the red-headed squirrel. I want you to do somethin' for me."

"What?"

"I want you to get Mrs. Wilder over here."

"Nope," Terry said, "won't do nothin' for you until I get my shoes back."

Josie laughed, "I got 'em back at the house. Walk back with me and I'll give 'em to you."

Terry laughed. "You think I'm stupid? I ain't walkin' back alone with you."

"What's wrong?" Josie winked. "Scared I'll make you disappear?"

"That I ain't afraid of," Terry said, "'cause I got your smelly disappearin' cream."

Josie's jaw dropped. "You stole my red-capped jar?"

"Didn't steal it. I borrowed it. Thought we might trade."

"Trade what?" Josie asked.

"My shoes for your stupid old disappearin' cream that doesn't work."

"Doesn't work?" Josie cackled. "You tried it?"

Terry nodded. "I tried to make my sister and this widow lady who wants to marry my pa disappear, but they're still around."

"Boy, you got spirit. Come 'round anytime and I'll have your shoes sittin' on the porch. Just give me back my rubbin' cream."

"Wait here," Terry said, running back to their wagon and reaching under the seat. He ran up to Josie and held out the jar. "You can have it if you do one other thing."

"What's that?" Josie asked.

"Take off the hex."

"Hex? What hex?"

"The hex you put on me when you cursed me."

"I didn't curse you or hex you," Josie protested.

"Yes you did, when you gave that toothless old man my shoes." Josie sighed. "Okay, here goes. You ready?"

Terry nodded.

"Hocus-pocus, reverse the worst, when I raise my hands I lift the curse!" She raised her arms and Terry blinked.

"Did you feel it go?" Josie asked, playfully.

"It's gone. I can feel it gone!" Terry shouted. "Everythin's sparkly," he said, giggling and jumping around. "It's like magic."

Josie laughed. "Does it feel like a hundred pounds been lifted off your back?"

"Yup."

"Does it feel like you can think clearer?" Josie asked.

"It sure does."

"Then the hex has been lifted. You're back to your normal tricky self again."

"Here's your cream," he said, tossing her the jar.

Josie barely caught it with her fingertips and chuckled as Terry skipped away. "Tell Mrs. Wilder I want to speak to her over here."

Terry shouted back. "She's up on the ridge, doin' some thinkin' my pa said."

Josie went back through the orchard and took the rough trail up to the top of the ridge. Laura was on her thinking rock, looking out over the Ozarks.

She sensed Josie's approach and turned, smiling. "I've been expecting you," Laura said.

"You knew I was comin'?" Josie asked.

"Just had this feeling that you'd be coming. I don't know why."

Josie sat down. "I was bringing some herb coughin' tea for the sick boy but Rutherford stopped me." Josie told her about the confrontation.

"Laura, you tell them that I want to help. My herbs don't produce instant miracles, but they sure do offer the beginning of the road to good health."

Laura looked at the old women in the patched dress. She was sincere in wanting to help, but she was clearly upset. Rutherford was getting to her. *He's getting to us all.*

As Laura listened, a chill went through her soul. *Something bad is going to happen. I can feel it.*

CHAPTER 29

A TIME FOR HEALING

By the end of the party, everyone had heard about the confrontations between Laura, Josie, and Rutherford. Speculation about the Flock and the death of Brother Bill was turning ugly.

Some sided against Josie, because she was old and different. Superstitions rooted deep in the hills were creeping across town like a fast-growing poisonous vine.

By the time of Sunday service, Rev. Youngun thought it best to put away his sermon on hope and promise and replace it with one from his heart. Here he was, a man of the cloth, and his own children believed in witches. *I've not done a proper job instructing them,* he worried.

Rev. Youngun looked over his congregation, prayed silently, then began. "We have a sickness in the hills, a sickness that is affecting all of us."

The congregation looked around uneasily, wondering what disease he was talking about.

"I'm not talking about a pox or plague, but it's a sickness just the same."

He looked around the room. "You have it . . . and you have it . . . and you have it," he said, pointing to nobody in particular, though they all felt he was pointing at them.

"It's a sickness that affects the way we think, talk, and live. It is a sickness of prejudice, superstition, and believing in myths and fairy tales—and it has gotten out of hand."

He paused, looking around. "There's an old woman of the hills, an old woman named Josie Tatum, who minds her own business. Doesn't hurt anyone. Matter of fact, from what I hear, she goes out of her way to help folks who are sick. But we joke and call her a witch.

"Is it because she doesn't go to church? Is it because she looks different or lives alone? Maybe it's because she raises herbs like your grandmothers did. But is that any reason to call her a witch? Since when are herbs evil?" he shouted.

" 'The earth is the Lord's, and the fulness thereof.' That's what it says in Psalm 24. We don't own this planet; we are assigned by God to take care of it. And one of the benefits of this caretaking is the herbs that spring forth."

He paused, looking around the room. "How many of you know that the Bible tells us to use herbs for good health? Read your Genesis; it's right there in the Bible. The Lord told Ezekiel that the fruit of the tree is for man's meat and the leaves for his medicine. Does that sound like witchcraft?"

Moving from behind the podium, he continued. "Do you call the counter lady at the pharmacy a witch because she dispenses medicines made from herbs? Do you call Dr. George a wizard if he gives you medicine made from plants and roots?

"Herbs have been with us from the beginning of time. Adam and Eve used herbs to treat their illnesses as have all people for thousands of years. Most of the people in the world continue to rely on them, yet are we so modern that we've turned our back on nature?"

He sighed. "There is no such thing as witches, but there is something called a sickness of the heart. It manifests itself in many ways. It might be callin' someone a name because they came from a different country, or making fun of the way they pray."

Raising his hands, he reached out to the room. "There are no witches, but there are evil people who knowingly spread lies and falsehoods. Let us ask for a time for healing, a healing of attitudes, and . . . a prayer for Abe Stern, the son of Mansfield's new rabbi."

CHAPTER 30

IGNORANT HILL WOMAN

Dr. George spent Monday morning with Abe, but wasn't able to find the cause of his coughing. He suspected the boy's lungs might have been damaged by the smallpox or from hiding in the dank basement for two years in Russia, but he wasn't sure.

"You know, Rabbi, I think that most good health is a matter of luck and common sense."

"Luck? What is lucky health?"

Dr. George smiled. "It all starts with your family history. That's kind of the luck of the draw, since we don't have much choice in the bein'-born department."

Rabbi Stern scoffed. "What does history have to do with health?"

"What I'm sayin' is that good luck is havin' long-livin' parents and grandparents. Bad luck is bein' in bad places that can affect your health."

Stern looked perplexed, so Dr. George continued. "Bein' in Russia during the troubled times and hidin' in that wet basement— that's a streak of bad luck."

He listened to Abe's chest again. "Yes sir, your family history tells you a lot. You got to look to your parents, grandparents, and even great-grandparents. If your ma and pa had some heart trouble, or some other organ problems, then chances are your body may have a weakness toward that."

"So you can . . . can do nothing?"

Dr. George smiled. "Good stock is what you're born with, but it's how you live your life which determines your health." He looked into Abe's eyes, then said, "Stick out your tongue . . . got some white spots."

While he checked Abe's ears, Dr. George said, "Next important thing is a good, commonsense diet. Good food strengthens the body, bad food and drink weakens it. It's that simple."

"You make all sound so easy," Rabbi Stern said.

"Eatin' right is easy," Dr. George replied.

"But when hungry, you'll eat anything," Rabbi Stern said, thinking back on the days hiding in the basement.

"That's a fact, but if you got a choice, then use your willpower and eat right."

Dr. George tapped Abe's knee. "You gonna run in the race, son?"

Abe smiled weakly. "I wish I could, but I feel so weak."

"You need to exercise to get your strength back up. If you can't race, maybe you can walk."

"But Abe's growing . . . growing . . ." He searched for the right word. "Weaker all the time," Rabbi Stern said.

"It could be from many things," Dr. George said, listening to Abe's chest for a third time. "He could even be allergic to something."

"Allergic? To what?"

"That's what the doctors in the big-city hospital can tell you."

"Should I take him Springfield?"

Dr. George shrugged. "They got a good hospital up there, but it's a fifteen-hour buggy ride, 'cause the next train to Springfield isn't till this weekend."

"I don't want to wait," Stern said, pacing impatiently. "Where other place can I take him?"

"I was going to say you could take the noon train to St. Louis. I could wire ahead to my old med school teacher and tell him that you were coming."

So Rabbi Stern took Abe to St. Louis and returned two days later.

The doctors told him that Abe had consumption, which was slowly killing a half-million other Americans. Or so they thought. They said to just keep Abe warm and off his feet.

The train ride back to Mansfield was depressing. Rabbi Stern didn't want to just give up. There had to be something he could do for his son.

Upon their return, Rabbi Stern learned that Josie had tried to bring some "mountain medicine" to their son at Laura's party, but that she'd been driven away by Rutherford. So he went to Apple Hill Farm and asked Laura about it, who confirmed the story.

"Is she doctor?" Stern asked.

Laura shrugged. "In the Ozarks, there are a lot of self-taught healers. Josie uses herbs like our grandparents did."

"But we have medicine, drugs to cure disease."

"Sometimes I think there are more side effects to using drugs and new medicines than we realize," Laura said. "Rabbi, there's big money, big money in selling medicine to get people into the medicine habit."

"But doctors—"

Laura interrupted. "I'm not telling you what to do. Josie's an herb healer, who dispenses as much common sense as she does medicine. I'd do what Dr. George says, but I wouldn't discount hearing Josie out. I kind of think common sense and good health go hand in hand."

"I should go see her?"

"Take Abe to see her and just hear her out."

"How I find this old woman?" the rabbi asked.

"I'll draw you a map. The walk will do you both good."

The only thing that Laura didn't tell him was that Rutherford had called Josie a witch. *There's no sense coloring the story any more,* she thought.

Abe spent the morning coughing and was too weak to walk, so his father carried him on his back. He trudged through the hills, following the map that Laura had given him to Josie's house.

Several times he had to stop and rest, closing his eyes to the memories. As Abe's health deteriorated, nightmares about hiding in the basement kept coming back to the rabbi.

He could see the panic in his wife's eyes, as the soldiers clashed outside, and the terror on Abe's face when he heard the neighbors being shot against the wall outside. It was a time of nightmares, living nightmares, when surviving meant closing your eyes, ears, and mind to the insanity just outside the root cellar.

But he couldn't close it off then, and he wasn't able to now. He was haunted—haunted by the feelings that he should have done something to save his neighbors and haunted by the thankfulness that his family survived.

Josie seemed to be expecting them and was waiting on the ridge. "Try puttin' the boy down and rest a bit. You're goin' to kill yourself." Abe didn't speak, he just kept eyeing Josie.

Rabbi Stern sat Abe on a rock and looked at the startlingly ugly old woman. "My name is—"

Josie waved him silent. "I know who you are and why you're here."

"I came for help for Abe."

Josie wiped the sweat off Abe's forehead. "Well, young fella, can you stand?"

Abe, who was fascinated by the old woman from the moment he saw her, nodded.

"Good, stand up." Abe got to his feet and stared at her face. "Cat got your tongue?" Josie asked.

Abe shook his head. "Are you the witch who took Terry's shoes?"

"Abe! Where your manners?" his father said.

Josie went wide-eyed, then burst out laughing. "You know that red-headed monkey?"

"He's my new friend," Abe said.

"Well, I hope your health's better than your choice in friends, but don't matter, come on," she said, trooping off toward her cabin.

Abe and his father followed behind, but as they neared the cabin, he had another coughing fit and had to be carried the rest of the way. Inside the cabin, Josie wiped Abe's brow again, then gave him some coughing tea. "Drink this."

"What's that?" Rabbi Stern asked, looking at the brown liquid.

Josie held up Abe's head for him to drink. "We got to stop his coughing 'fore we can do anything."

"But what is in drink?"

"Coughing tea. It's got blue violet, horehound, hyssop, rosemary, and black cohosh."

Abe drank the tea and closed his eyes.

Josie smiled. "You got to clean and purify the system before you can figure out what's wrong. He could have all kinds of things blockin' him up."

Stern shook his head. "In Russia, they used leeches to do that."

"This ain't Russia. I just believe that you got to put the body in tune with itself. That by itself can stop most asthma or bronchial coughs."

Abe's cough stopped and he drifted off to sleep. Josie motioned for Stern to follow her to the front porch. "Now tell me what those big-city doctors told you in St. Louis."

"They said he has consumption. They will send medicine, that he should stay quiet, not move around much."

Josie snorted. "Ain't much of a prescription for a young boy. Sounds like they're talkin' 'bout him dyin'."

Stern nodded gravely. "They said half-million people year die of this consumption, many of them children."

Josie poured herself a glass of "vitality tea" and sat back, rocking. "Tell me 'bout Russia. That's one place I've never been to."

"You have traveled a lot?" Rabbi Stern asked, eyeing her clothes.

"Not a whole bunch. Been to Springfield once but that's 'bout it. That was enough travelin' for me. So I travel by readin' about places. Now tell me about Russia."

So Stern told his story. About hiding in the basement, the small-pox, eating rat bread and grass while they hid from the soldiers.

"Tell me that part again about eatin' grass," Josie said, leaning forward.

Rabbi Stern blushed. "It was just way to keep Abe alive."

"But you say it sometimes made him feel better?" Stern nodded. Josie sighed. "What kind of grass was it he was eatin'?"

Stern shrugged. "Grass, just grass, what was around house."

"What kind of grass?" she asked.

"What you need to know that for?"

Josie coughed and sipped her tea. "Rabbi, I don't tell you how to run your religion, so don't be tellin' me how to run my herb practice. Do you know what kind of grass you were chewin'?"

"No."

"You think Abe would remember?"

"How could he? He was just young boy and—"

"The mind can remember smells and tastes like you wouldn't believe. You said Abe was well for a while when he ate the grass?"

"I thought so. Or maybe I hoped so."

Josie stood up. "Go wake the boy and bring him out here. Let's see if he can remember what kind of grass he was eatin'."

Taking Abe by the arm, Josie walked him around what was left of her gardens. "Was this the kind of grass you ate in Russia?" she asked.

Abe sniffed the grass and made a face. "It wasn't that."

"Hmm," Josie said, picking up another pot. "Was this the kind?"

Abe sniffed it and shook his head. "No, it smelled different."

At the end of the garden, a small doe was chewing on a pot of grass. "Get out of here, you're eatin' my medicine chest," she shouted out.

Abe giggled. "Medicine chest? This is a garden."

Josie took him by the hand. "What grows here is what I think can help you get better."

"You mean like what that deer was eating?" Abe asked playfully.

Josie nodded. "He was eatin' up my pot of wheatgrass which . . ." She paused, then tugged Abe along. "Come on over here and smell this."

She pulled off a clump of the wheatgrass and held it to Abe's nose. "Smell it."

Abe took a deep breath and closed his eyes. "This is what we ate!"

Josie pulled a couple of handfuls and handed them to Abe. "Start eatin'."

"You want him eat grass? Like animal?" his father asked.

"Rabbi, it saved him once and it might just save him again." She put a handful up to Abe's mouth. "Bite it, eat it like a rabbit."

Rabbi Stern shook his head. "Grass for animals."

Josie laughed. "Cows intuitively go to the pasture grass that's best for what ails 'em. Cats and dogs eat wheatgrass when they're sick. Nature's always callin' to us if we'll just listen."

Josie went back into the house and packed up a sack of herbs. "Here's some chickweed, golden seal, slippery elm, coltsfoot, and a jar of honey."

Rabbi Stern listened politely as she told him how to make herb tea but was thinking, *She is old ignorant hill woman. Eat grass. This is not right. I swore we'd never eat grass and rats again,* he thought. *I am a rabbi. I believe in doctors and medicine. What am I doing here?*

He didn't notice that Abe had eaten almost the entire garden pot of wheatgrass and seemed ravenous for more. As they left her cabin, Josie felt pleased. "Have him drink that tea every day and eat as much wheatgrass as you can find."

"Anything else?" Stern asked.

"Oh, I almost forgot. Give me a moment." Josie went back inside her cabin, then returned with a long string of garlic. "Abe might be sufferin' from eatin' that rat bread."

"How?" Stern asked.

"Might have intestinal worms. Worms will weaken you, make you so you can't hardly run or walk."

Abe made a face. "Worms in my stomach?"

"Might be," Josie said, shrugging. "Just eat this garlic mixed in your other food and have your pa check your droppin's."

On the way back, Abe smiled. "She can help me, can't she?"

Rabbi Stern looked at the strange assortment of leaves and roots, and shook his head. It reminded him of the folk doctors in Russia, whom he was taught not to trust. "I think we wait for medicine. Doctors know what is best for you."

"But Josie said—"

His father silenced him. "I know best. You will wait to take doctor's medicine."

CHAPTER 31

THE CURE?

Laura had agreed to meet Stern at Mom's Cafe to discuss what Josie had told him. "But Miss Laura," he protested, "she told him eat grass and garlic!"

"Maybe the wheatgrass is what Abe survived on in Russia."

"And maybe not," Stern said. "And garlic can cause stomach-aches."

Laura laughed. "I don't know what you put in your kosher cooking, but garlic is something I know about. It's a natural septic for the body. It cleanses your tracts of germs and helps the blood, and is good for asthma."

"But it smells bad!"

"Rabbi, you got nothing to lose by letting Abe try it," Laura said.

Customers in Mom's Cafe were eavesdropping on their conversation, so Laura lowered her tone. "You want Abe to get better, don't you? Let him eat the wheatgrass."

Outside, a group of kids raced by, practicing for Saturday's big race. "I just wish Abe were healthy, like those children."

"He'll get better."

"I just wish we had consumption medicine from doctors in St. Louis. That will cure Abe."

While Stern and Laura talked, Terry skipped down Main Street toward Abe's house. He found his friend, sitting on the front porch, wrapped in a blanket.

"Why are you all wrapped up? It ain't cold," Terry said.

Abe sighed. "Father says I have consumption and need to keep warm."

Terry looked at the sweat on Abe's brow. "You got a fever?"

"Don't think so."

"Then take off that blanket before you sweat to death."

"Okay," Abe said, standing up.

"Phewee, your breath stinks!" Terry exclaimed.

Abe giggled. "I've been eating garlic."

"You don't have to tell me!" Terry said, scrunching his nose.

Abe told Terry about going to see Josie and about her giving him wheatgrass and garlic to eat, and that his father didn't want him to.

"Then why are you eatin' it?" Terry asked.

"Because I want to get better, so I can run and play with you."

Terry reached into his pocket and pulled out some gum. "You better chew on this."

"Why?"

" 'Cause one whiff of your death-breath and your pa'll know for sure that you been disobeyin' him."

Abe put the stick of gum in his mouth and began chewing. "Where you learn so much?"

Terry put a stick in his mouth. "So much what?"

"You seem to have answer for everything," Abe sighed.

Terry shrugged. "Just born smart, I reckon. You want to come and play?"

"Don't think I better. Father said he'd be back in one hour."

"He'll never know. Let's go peek and see if we can see Old Fred. It's Friday the 13th."

"Old Fred?" Abe asked.

"You don't know about Old Fred? The dead man who hanged himself and became a ghost?"

Abe shook his head.

"Well, this bein' the most unluckiest day of all, let me tell you the story I learned years ago when I was little." Terry told Abe what he'd learned from Maurice the week before and about the dare.

"What is a dare?" Abe asked.

Terry thought for a moment. "A dare is a challenge, sort of a test."

"Do you think this Maurice was serious."

"He says he was kiddin', but I think he was just tellin' us that to keep us away from the treasure."

"You wouldn't be scared to go into haunted house?"

"No problem," Terry said, puffing out his chest. "We're the Younguns. We ain't scared of nothin'."

Terry caught Josie coming across the field from the corner of his eye and started to leave. He still thought she *might* be a witch.

"Where you going?" Abe asked.

"Got to run. See ya'."

Josie wanted to check on Abe and brought along more wheat-grass, garlic, and another batch of coughing tea she brewed up.

"You feelin' any better?" she asked.

"You scared me," Abe said.

"Well, don't go gettin' all nervous. I just came to see how you're feelin' and bring you some more wheatgrass and garlic." She caught something in Abe's glance. "You been eatin' it, ain't you?"

Abe looked down. "My father doesn't believe in your woods medicine."

"And what do you believe?"

Abe looked up. "I don't know. I know the grass has made me feel better and garlic did what you said."

"So you been disobeyin' your pa," she said, cackling. "There's hope for the future yet."

"Did you hear what I said?" Abe asked.

"You said you found some wigglies."

Abe scratched his head. "Wigglies? I said that the garlic did what you said it would."

"Wigglies. You found some worms, didn't you?"

"How did you know what to give me?" Abe blushed.

Josie sighed. "Been treatin' folks with herbs and common sense all my life. I've seen a lot of young boys lose their energy to worms. Keep eatin' the garlic and it'll drive all the worms out of you."

"I remember eating grass in Russia. It doesn't taste bad."

"Wouldn't matter if it tasted like eatin' old train tickets. If it helps you, it tastes great," Josie said, grinning. "Is your pa here?"

"He's at the cafe with Mrs. Wilder."

"Well, here's some more medicine. Drink a glass of this tea, three times a day, and you'll start endin' that cough."

Josie patted him on the head, then turned to leave. "I'll be back soon."

Abe sat quietly by himself, not knowing that Jackson Rutherford was standing across the road, watching him. He looked to the sky and thought, *I feel something toward that boy. I think I'm being called to cleanse him.*

Seeing Rabbi Stern walking toward the house, Rutherford walked out and stood in front of him.

"Can I help you?" Stern asked.

Rutherford stared intensely. "It is *I* who can help you."

"What is it?"

Rutherford gripped his staff. "I want to cure your son."

"Are you a doctor?" Stern asked.

"I am a healer; I can cleanse the body of the evils that afflict it."

Rabbi Stern's eyes brightened. "What kind of medicine do you use?"

"Trust me Jewish man. We are brothers of the same cloth."

Sensing something was strange about this man, he reached out his hand. "I am Rabbi Stern and my son is—"

"Abe, short for Abraham. A name from the Bible."

"And what is your name?" Stern asked.

"I am Jackson Rutherford, leader of the Flock, sent to heal your son—heal him tonight."

Suddenly, Abe began coughing violently on the front porch. "I have to help my son," Stern said, running off.

Rutherford called after him, "It is I who can help him. Only I."

It took several minutes to bring Abe's cough under control. Stern didn't even notice that Rutherford was standing beside him. "What do you want?"

Rutherford smiled. "I want to cure your son. I have had a vision." Then his eyes went wide. "What is this?" he said, pushing the basket of wheatgrass and garlic away from him.

"Josie brought it to me," Abe whispered.

Stern frowned. "She was here?"

"She is evil. She's a witch," Rutherford snapped.

Stern gave Rutherford a look of disgust. "Enough talk. I want you to leave. You're the man that people are whispering about."

Rutherford tapped his staff twice, then touched it to Abe's feet. "Your son is goin' to die unless he's cleansed of the evil that's in him."

"Leave my house," Stern said.

"You cannot stop the signs," Rutherford said coldly, and he turned to go back to the Flock.

CHAPTER 32

ESCAPE

Sit down!" Rutherford ordered.

Susan resisted. "Let me go. I want to leave the Flock."

"You need to be cleansed, so I can marry you," he said, shaking her.

With her eyes glaring, Susan said coldly, "I will never marry you. Not on my grave!"

Brother Robert carried in the crate and kicked it. Judgment's tail started buzzing. "You have to be sleep cleansed. That is the way. I cannot cure the boy until you are cleansed."

"What boy?"

"The Jewish boy is of no consequence to you. But I have had a vision that we are to be married at sundown. That is the way."

Susan tried to run, but Brother Robert grabbed her. "That is not my way," she shouted.

Rutherford lifted up the lid of the crate and then went to Susan. "You are to lie down and sleep, right here," he said, pointing to the blanket on the floor. If the snake doesn't bother you, then you will be ready."

Susan turned and saw Judgment sticking his head up through the crate. Brother Robert nodded. "Judgment only bites those with the signs."

Rutherford shook his head in agreement. "Yes, the snake looks for signs. It roots out evil."

Susan forced her body to calm down and hesitantly sat on the blanket. *I wonder if a snake gets a taste for human blood? I wonder if it gets to like killing people?* she asked herself.

"Momma! Momma!" her son Tyler screamed out, running into the barn.

"Get that boy out!" Rutherford ordered.

Her daughter, Carrie, came behind her brother, screaming, "Leave Momma alone!"

Rutherford picked the girl up and carried her to the door. He turned and said to Susan, "Sleep tight. And say your prayers."

Susan laid her head down, pretending to be calm. "Now I lay me down to sleep I—" She stopped as the door closed.

Judgment slithered out from the crate and came toward her. Susan sat up, frozen in place, watching the snake. Judgment coiled up in front of her and shot his tongue in and out.

Then a rat scampered in the corner and he shot toward the sound. Susan walked quietly to the barn door and looked out through the crack. Her two children were sitting on a log across from the barn, away from the Flock. Rutherford was preaching about his latest vision on the other side.

Susan started to slide the door open, then felt a nudging against her side. She turned and went cold. Judgment's head was tapping against her leg! He had a big, dead rat in his mouth.

Trying not to panic, Susan waited until the snake had swallowed the rat, then curled up to let it digest. She carefully worked the door open, then crept toward her children at the edge of the clearing.

Tyler saw her and started to speak, but she silenced him with a finger to her lips. She motioned for him and Carrie to follow her, and they crawled behind the log to where she was hiding.

"It's time to go," she whispered to them.

"But where are we going, Momma?" Carrie asked.

"I met a woman in the woods. Her name is Laura. She'll know what to do."

"I'm so hungry, Momma," Tyler said.

"Me, too," Carrie said.

"She looked like a good woman. She'll feed us," Susan said.

As they slipped away into the woods, Brother Robert went back to check on Susan and found her gone. Rutherford was enraged.

"She won't go far without her children," he said.

One of the Flock shouted out, "She's taken them!"

Rutherford raised his fist to the sky. "We must find her before she hurts the Flock! Evil tongues can bring down mighty forces if they are not cut off."

Brother Robert and two others headed along the road to town, and others in the Flock searched the perimeter for clues to Susan's direction. Rutherford set off on horseback, following his instincts.

Susan and the children were able to keep ahead of him, running along the rough trail and edging down the ravine cliffs. Rutherford found a broken branch here and there and knew where they were heading: Apple Hill Farm.

At the edge of the cliff, he gazed toward the Wilder's farm and caught a glimpse of them running through the orchards. "So they run to the witch's house. Evil draws evil," he said to the horse, kicking hard to spur him on.

Laura was in the kitchen when she heard the soft knock on the door. "Yes?"

There was no answer.

Thinking it was another of Rutherford's tricks, she walked guardedly toward it. She found Susan Ponder and her two children standing there.

"Can I help you?" Laura asked, startled at their disheveled appearance.

"We need help, bad," Susan said.

Laura opened the door. "Are you here alone?"

Susan nodded. "He'll be comin'."

"Who?"

"Rutherford. Jackson Rutherford. He wants to marry me and—" Susan broke down in tears.

Laura brought them into the kitchen and sat them down. "Calm down, calm down."

Susan peered out the window. "I know he's coming. He won't rest until I've been sleep cleansed."

"You're safe now."

Susan was on the verge of hysteria. "He said he had to marry me before he could cure a sick boy."

"A sick boy? Who?"

Susan wiped her eyes. "He didn't say. Just had that look in his eyes."

Laura was not prepared for all this but looked at the scruffy children. "Are you kids hungry?"

They nodded.

"What would you like to eat?"

"Food," Tyler answered.

"What kind of food," Laura asked, smiling.

"It don't matter," Susan said. "They're so hungry they're practically starved to death."

Laura pointed to the icebox. "Take what you want."

While Tyler and Carrie gorged themselves, Susan told her story. She told everything. About Judgment, the people who died in Georgia, how her husband died—about the signs and the rituals.

It was an amazing story that Laura would have found hard to believe if she hadn't experienced Rutherford herself. So she stood up and went to the phone.

When the operator came on, Laura said, "Clara, this is Laura Ingalls Wilder. Get me Sheriff Peterson—fast."

Peterson said he would come out right away. Laura turned to Susan and smiled. "The sheriff's coming."

They both heard the horse at the same time and looked out. Rutherford was coming up fast. Susan began moaning and the kids hugged her legs.

"Momma, don't let him take us back," Tyler whimpered.

Rutherford reared his horse up and shouted, "I know she's in there!"

"Don't tell him we're here. Please," Susan whispered.

"You're safe here," Laura said. "Manly will be back soon and the sheriff's coming."

Tears rimmed Susan's eyes. Laura was frightened of Rutherford but had to give strength to Susan and her children. "I'll handle him. Don't you worry."

She walked out onto the front porch. "What do you want?"

"I want my woman and the children," Rutherford demanded.

"Get off my property," Laura said coldly.

"I ain't leavin' without them."

Laura shrugged. "Suit yourself. I called the sheriff and told him all about how Bill Ponder died."

"No one will believe a crazy woman like that grieving widow. And no one will believe a witch's friend."

"Then wait and see," Laura said, crossing her arms. "I know that the sheriff thinks something's been going on, and my husband's out in the barn, cleaning his shotgun. Maybe you ought to talk to him and those two barrels," she said, hoping the bluff would work.

Laura walked to the edge of the porch and shouted, pretending that Manly was in the barn. "Manly, bring that shotgun out here and talk to this trespasser."

Rutherford glared. "You will get yours. Mark my words."

With that, he galloped off through the orchards. At the top of the hill, he came upon Josie. "Out of my way, witch!" he screamed, knocking her down with his horse. Josie fell backward, hitting her head on the rocks.

At the edge of the ridge, he found Brother Robert. "Go get the boy. Now!" he ordered. "It is time to prove my power."

Brother Robert nodded and headed toward Abe's house.

Laura found Josie unconscious in the orchards and used creek water to bring her back around. "Are you all right?" Laura asked softly.

Josie nodded, rubbing the bump on the back of her head. "Just came by to tell you that the rabbi's boy is gonna get better. Think he's got congestion and worms. That's what's makin' him weak."

Susan came out and helped Laura lift Josie to her feet. "What are you doin' here?" Josie asked suspiciously. "You're one of the Flock, ain't you?"

"Susan came here with her children," Laura said, "to escape from that Rutherford. He's got a crazy idea of marrying her."

"Marrying?" Josie exclaimed.

"He's tryin' to force me," Susan whispered.

Laura nodded. "He tried to cleanse her with a snake first."

"You didn't get bit?" Josie asked.

Susan shook her head. "I escaped when Rutherford left the barn. He's had a vision of curing that boy you're talkin' about. Thinks it'll show his great power."

"Abe? How do you know it's the same boy?" Josie asked.

"I heard you say 'rabbi's boy.' Rutherford said he had a vision of curing a Jewish boy."

"Cure? What kind of cure?" Laura asked.

"Snake cure," Susan said, looking down.

Josie shook her head. "I got to get goin'," she said, running off quickly.

"Where are you going?" Laura called after her.

"You stay here with that woman and the kids. I got to go to that boy."

"The sheriff's coming," Laura shouted. "Let him handle it."

"Like he did the last one?" Josie shouted back.

CHAPTER 33

BURN THE WITCH!

Tamara Stern put Abe in bed for the night, knowing that sleep would do him good. When her husband went to the printing shed to work on the Yiddish machine, she thought she heard something upstairs.

She stopped to listen and heard footsteps on the back stairs. Frightened, thinking back on the soldiers in Russia, she hesitated. When she regained control of herself, she crept to the back and saw a man holding Abe.

"Mother, help me!" Abe blurted out, managing to get Brother Robert's hand off his mouth.

"What are you doing?" she screamed.

"He is going to be cured," Brother Robert said, putting his hand back over Abe's mouth. As he ran from the house, Tamara screamed.

In the printing shed, Rabbi Stern was working on the type for his first edition.

"Abe . . . Abe's been taken!" she screamed, as she ran into the printing room.

Stern turned off the press. "I couldn't hear you. What did you say?"

"A man took Abe. Said he was going to cure him."

"What? Where did they go?"

Stern ran to the backyard, but in the twilight it was hard to see anything.

"Where are you going?" she asked, as he ran back to the house.

"To call Sheriff Peterson."

But the sheriff wasn't in. He was on his way to Apple Hill Farm.

Stern had the operator connect him to the Wilder's. He was in a panic by this point. "Laura, Laura. Someone's stolen Abe!"

"Slow down, Rabbi."

"My wife saw man take Abe. Said he was going to cure him."

"Oh Lord," Laura said, shaking her head. "It's got to be Rutherford."

"Who?" Stern said, as the line began to crackle.

"Jackson Rutherford. A fanatic who lives with a group of families he calls the Flock. He fancies himself a healer."

"Where this place?" he shouted, trying to be heard over the static.

"At the old Williams place," Laura shouted. "About two miles up the north road. Look for a tree that lightning split."

Manly entered the kitchen. "What's goin' on?"

"Rutherford's taken Abe," Laura said, waiting for the static to clear on the line.

Laura noticed Manly's raised eyebrows when he saw Susan and her children and quickly added, "And this is Susan Ponder and her two children. They've come to stay with us for a while."

The static was too much for Stern, so he slammed the phone down and got in his wagon.

"Where are you going?" his wife asked.

"I am going to get Abe," he said. "Stay by the phone till the sheriff calls."

Though the rabbi was unsure of the area, he took the north road out of town. As twilight came on, heat lightning crackled in the air, making him shiver.

Brother Robert carried Abe into the barn. Rutherford took him into his arms. "Why is he not speaking?"

"Boy had a coughing fit on the way over. I thought his insides were comin' out," Brother Robert said.

Rutherford looked into Abe's vacant eyes. "This boy needs to be cleansed. I feel his soul passing."

Brother Robert shook his head. "I think he's just coughed out. He'll come back around."

Rutherford wouldn't listen. "Get the Flock in. We must cleanse him now."

By the time Rabbi Stern came to the blackened tree split by the first lightning of spring, he could hear the chanting of the Flock. The repetitious murmur and the shadows of the night gave him goose bumps.

Looking up, he said, "God, please keep Abe safe. Take me instead."

He parked his wagon to the side and approached the barn cautiously. The flickering lights through the cracks in the walls made the barn look like a prism.

He peeked in cautiously and saw Rutherford holding Abe in his arms. He was chanting with the Flock as another man brought Judgment's crate in from the back room.

What is he doing? Stern wondered. *What's in the crate? What should I do?*

Behind him, Josie was watching from the woods. She arrived as Stern was parking his wagon and decided to wait. She didn't know who was who in the dark, but she knew the boy was inside.

When Stern stood up and opened the barn door, she crept closer to look through the wall cracks. The Flock turned to face the rabbi.

Rutherford looked around with anger in his eyes. "Keep chanting! Keep chanting!" He stared at Stern. "Rabbi, what do you want?"

"I want my son."

"He is sick and needs to be healed," Rutherford said, looking down at Abe.

"That's what doctor's for," Stern said coldly.

The Flock chanted louder as Rutherford stamped his foot. Then he handed Abe to Brother Robert. "Take him into the back room and lay him down."

Stern stepped forward. "Give Abe to me!"

Rutherford wheeled around. "Not until he's cleansed!"

Stern walked through the chanting Flock, parting them with his arms. But he was unable to get to Abe before Brother Robert carried him from the room.

Rutherford reached into the crate and lifted Judgment out. "He will cure your son, Rabbi." The rattler's tail echoed dangerously, blending with the chanting.

"It is time. Time for Judgment," Rutherford said.

Stern saw the distant look in Rutherford's eyes. "Snake . . . Judgment . . . are you insane?" Stern asked, stunned by what he was witnessing.

"Come here, Rabbi. Come meet Judgment," Rutherford said, motioning to him.

Outside, Josie shook her head. "Got to do something," she mumbled.

Creeping along the side of the barn, she looked into the room where Brother Robert had taken Abe. He was lying there, half-asleep, on a pile of old burlap sacks. Brother Robert was standing guard.

Rutherford called from the barn. "Brother Robert, come back here. Help me get the snake ready. I think I see the signs."

Josie watched Brother Robert walk back into the barn, leaving Abe alone. Josie shrugged, thinking, *Guess this is my sign to do something.*

She tried the door to the room, but it had a rusty old drop latch in place. Wiggling didn't work, so she took the straight pin holding the hem of her skirt in place and opened the latch.

Josie crept to Abe's side. "Come on, son, we got to get outta here."

Abe turned and blinked. "What? Who? Oh, it's you, Josie."

"We don't got time for a long hello. That man's gonna hurt you if we don't move now."

Abe tried to stand but was too weak.

"You been eatin' the wheatgrass and garlic?" she asked.

He started to cough again, but Josie cupped his mouth. "Just tell your mind that you ain't gonna cough now," she whispered. "We can't have them hearin' you." With a deep sigh, she picked Abe up like a baby and put him over her shoulder.

"Where you taking me?" Abe asked.

"Home. If these old bones will take us," she grunted, taking the first step.

"To my home? To my mother?" he asked.

"Nope," Josie said. She didn't notice the small wrapped bundle of herbs fall from her pocket. "We're goin' to my home. Gonna get you better."

As she walked off into the darkness, carrying the weak boy, Abe asked, "Are you gonna feed me kosher herbs?"

"Kosher herbs?" she said, chuckling. "All Mother Nature's herbs are kosher!"

Inside the barn, Rutherford was lost in a trance, walking among the Flock. Stern felt as if he might faint when he saw Judgment, but he kept his head. He had to save Abe.

Rutherford tossed Judgment up and down. "Go get the boy! It is the time!"

Brother Robert left the room, then came running back. "He's gone."

Rutherford held Judgment with one hand. "Gone? He was too weak to run away."

Brother Robert shook his head. "I think he had help," he said, holding out the packet of herbs that Josie had dropped.

Rutherford took the herbs in his hand and turned to the Flock. "It is the calling card of the witch. It is time to rid the mountains of the evil."

The Flock lined up against the walls as Rutherford walked toward them. "Brother Robert, get the torches. We are going to burn the witch out. We will finish what was left undone in Salem."

Stern grabbed Rutherford's arm. "You can't do that! My son is with her!"

"Rabbi," Rutherford said slowly, "there is a reason for everything that happens." He handed Judgment to Brother Robert and picked up his staff.

"There is no reason, no reason to do this," Stern shouted.

Rutherford knocked him down with the staff.

"You cannot stop my vision."

Stern tried to get up but was clubbed down. Blood trickled down his forehead. "You are crazy."

Rutherford looked down. "What is crazy is letting witches live." Turning in a half-circle, he shouted to the Flock, "It is time. Tonight we burn the witch out! Brother Robert, bring Judgment."

Stern watched as the lanterns were lit and the torches wrapped. *This is insanity,* he thought to himself, left alone in the darkness. *I've got to get help. I've got to get to the sheriff.* Then he remembered. *He's at Apple Hill Farm.*

Outside, the Flock was praying with Rutherford, seeking the signs. Stern slipped into the shadows and followed the moonlight toward Laura's house.

Josie hoped that Rutherford would think that Abe had gone home. *There's no way he'll know I was there,* she thought.

Stopping to rest, Josie set Abe down. "How you feelin', honey child?"

"I'm okay," he whispered. "Are we almost there?"

"Almost," she said, standing back up. "Just that you're kinda heavy and I'm kinda old."

"You need to eat more kosher herbs," Abe smiled.

"You're gonna be all right," Josie said, kissing his forehead.

Across the ravine, Laura was trying to calm Manly down. He was furious that Rutherford had come, threatening Laura, Susan, and the children on his own property. "I got to go over there, Laura," Manly said. "That boy might be there."

Laura shook her head. "The sheriff will be here any minute. Bad enough that Josie's somewhere out there with a banged-up head. I don't need you hurt. I need you here protecting us."

"Laura, Manly, you home?" the sheriff called out from the front porch.

"Come on in, Sheriff," Manly said. "We're in the kitchen."

"Will someone tell me what all's happenin'?" he asked, coming into the kitchen.

Laura shook her head. "Susan escaped from that man Rutherford. She says he killed her husband with a big snake."

"Killed him? How?"

Susan spoke up. "He uses the big rattlesnake, Judgment, for cleansing. He's crazy."

"Things have gotten worse," Laura said.

"Worse? What could be worse?" the sheriff asked.

"Someone took the rabbi's son. I think it was Rutherford."

Suddenly, Rabbi Stern burst through the kitchen door. He was covered with briars and cut from the thorns.

"Sheriff . . . Sheriff . . . you've got to stop them," he said, gasping, trying to catch his breath.

Sheriff Peterson helped him to a chair. "Slow down there, Rabbi. Tell me what's happened."

"Rutherford had Abe at barn. Had crazy idea of using big snake to cure him."

"Did you leave him there?" Susan cried out.

Stern shook his head. "The old woman, Josie, sneaked in and carried Abe away."

"Good for Josie," Laura said. "He's in good hands now."

Stern shook his head back and forth. "No, no, no! They've gone after her to burn her out."

"Burn her out?" the sheriff asked.

Stern nodded. "They said to burn witch out."

Sheriff Peterson turned to Manly. "What's the fastest way to Josie's from here?"

"The north road is the easiest and then up through Simon's Wash," Manly said.

"That's the long way," Laura said.

"What's the fastest?" the sheriff asked.

"On horseback through the ravines," she said.

The sheriff whistled. "Mighty dangerous at night."

"She's right; it's the fastest way," Manly said. "Come on, let's saddle up in the barn." They left Susan and the children in the house with orders to keep the doors locked.

With only the moonlight to guide them, Laura, Manly, Rabbi Stern, and the sheriff headed out toward Josie's cabin. Each of them knew that they were on a desperate race against time, hoping against hope that they wouldn't be guided by the torching of her cabin.

At the crest of the ridge, near her thinking rock, Laura pulled up her horse. The Ozarks were washed in the light of the moon.

"Why're you stoppin'?" Manly shouted.

"I'm worried that the rabbi won't be able to keep up along the trail."

"I hold on until my son is safe," Stern said defiantly.

"Look over there!" Manly pointed.

At the far end of the adjoining ridge, a torch was lit. Then a second. Then a third.

"They're takin' the ridge tops. Probably goin' to toss the torches down on her cabin," Peterson said. He turned to Manly and Laura. "Manly, you and Laura take the ravines and I'll ride up along the ridge to try and stop 'em."

"What about me?" Stern said.

Peterson shrugged. "You come with me. Just be careful, 'cause we'll be ridin' along the edge at some points."

Just a mile away, Rutherford quieted his followers. In the flickering torchlight, he raised his staff.

"Tonight, we will remove evil from the woods so that we can truly build our paradise on earth."

The Flock nodded, lifting their torches higher.

"We are going to take back this land for the good and the righteous. That is the vision I have had."

"What about the boy?" Brother Robert asked.

"If she won't give him up, then so be it. He will burn too," Rutherford said. "That is the way of the vision. Let's go!"

Josie sat in her cabin, exhausted. Carrying Abe had nearly killed her. It was a relief to close the door, to shut out the night. She had no idea that Rutherford was closing in on her.

"These old bones are tired, Abe."

"I dropped my yarmulke," Abe said, feeling around on his head.

"You'll survive," Josie said, gasping for breath.

"But my head's got to stay covered," Abe protested.

Josie looked around and found a round pot holder. "Put this on."

"But it's not black. I've never heard of plaid yarmulke."

Josie laughed. "Call it an Ozark special."

Abe coughed, then gagged. "I'm feeling sick from all the jostling."

Josie poured him a glass of her energy sun tea. "Drink some of this. It should calm your stomach down while I get you something to eat."

She chopped up garlic and some greens and handed it to Abe. "Eat."

"But the worms came out," he protested.

"You got to eat the garlic every day until you don't see any worms for two weeks," she said, heading toward the door.

Abe looked around the strange cabin, with all the hanging herbs and sticks. "Where you going?"

"I ain't leavin'. I'm just goin' out to get you some more wheatgrass. I got to get your body cleansed out good."

"Cleansed. That's what that man in the barn said."

Josie shrugged. "What he said and I'm doin' are two different things."

The moon was beautiful. Josie couldn't help but admire the star-filled heavens. She breathed in deeply. *Tomorrow will begin better days for everyone. The sheriff can handle Rutherford and Abe will begin healing and—*

"There's the witch," echoed a chillingly familiar voice.

Josie looked toward the top of the ridge above her home. Rutherford stood out, surrounded by his torch-carrying followers.

"In the name of goodness, burn her out!" Rutherford screamed.

Laura guided her horse through the narrow ravine trail. Even in daylight it was a hard path to follow on foot. On horseback in the dark, it was dangerous.

Though the moon was full, moving clouds cast everything into darkness without warning. Manly shouted from behind, "Laura, slow down! Wait until the clouds pass."

Laura shook her head. "We've got to hurry, Manly."

The landscape of the night played tricks on her mind. The rocks she had walked on during the day became shapeless, eerie piles, shrouded in the patch quilt of moonlight.

The ravine path was the shortest way to Josie's, but what was familiar during the day became the unknown in the dark. Laura concentrated on remembering the moonlight-covered landmarks that marked the turning points.

"Oh, Lord," she cried out as her horse stumbled, perilously close to a steep drop. But he quickly regained his footing.

"Watch yourself," Manly shouted. "One fall and you're dead."

The sheriff and Rabbi Stern galloped along the ridge tops. The rabbi had never really mastered the art of horseback riding and was holding on for dear life as they jumped logs and rocks.

"Hold on, Rabbi," the sheriff shouted. He turned to show encouragement. "It gets rough up ahead."

Before he could turn back around, Sheriff Peterson was knocked off his horse by a low-hanging tree limb. Rabbi Stern jerked his horse to a halt and climbed off.

"Are you all right?" he asked, listening to the hoofbeats of the sheriff's horse running off in panic.

The sheriff was knocked almost unconscious. "Ride on ahead, Rabbi. I'll follow behind on foot."

"Are you sure? There's blood on your face."

Peterson laughed painfully. "Must've hit that limb pretty hard. Now you go on ahead. Your son needs you."

Stern reluctantly mounted up, and the sheriff struggled to his feet. "Take the trail straight and you can't miss it. But don't go over the cliff 'cause it's about a fifty-foot drop to her cabin."

Peterson looked around. "Dang, must have lost my hat somewhere around here."

The rabbi took off his black bowler hat and put it on the sheriff's head. It slipped down over his ears. "But it's your hat," the sheriff protested.

Rabbi Stern nodded. "I've got my little hat on," he smiled, patting his yarmulke.

The sheriff slapped the rabbi's horse, spurring him forward. "God be with you," he shouted.

"He always is," the rabbi shouted back.

In the ravines, Laura and Manly were going as fast as they dared. The path seemed to wind more than she remembered. *Like a snake,* she thought, and she shuddered.

A long string of clouds blocked the moonlight. *The brush seems too thick here. Is this the way?* Laura panicked for a moment. *Have they reached Josie's house yet?*

When the clouds passed, the rocks around her took on shapes of demons. *They're not real,* Laura thought to herself. *It's just my imagination.*

Laura used the moonlight as a guide, hoping that she hadn't missed any of the turns she knew by heart on her walks. But soon the moonlight was gone and she felt lost.

"Burn the witch! Burn the witch!" echoed through the ravines. *Oh, God, please don't let them hurt her.*

Then the moonlight returned and she saw the split through the rocks. *Josie's cabin is just ahead!*

Josie slammed the cabin door and bolted it. "What's wrong?" cried Abe. "Who's out there?"

Josie put her weight to the door. "It's him—the man with the snake."

Abe began shaking and hugged himself, then started to cough. Josie laid him down on her bed and covered him with her quilt.

"Come out, witch!" Rutherford cried.

Rutherford and the Flock had descended the ridge and were approaching the cabin.

Holding up the big snake, Rutherford called out to Josie. "If you're not an evil one, come out and be cleansed. That will prove me wrong."

Josie shouted out from the cabin. "Leave us alone. We want no part of your doin's."

"Brother Robert," Rutherford said quietly, "burn the witch's garden. Maybe that'll make her come out."

The remains of her garden went up in flames, crackling in the night. Josie looked out, then walked over to Abe.

"Don't leave me," he moaned.

"I ain't gonna leave you, honey. But if I stay in here, you're gonna get hurt. So I gotta go out and talk to that crazy man to keep them from hurtin' you."

Slipping off the old, thick bolt, Josie shouted, "I'm comin' out to talk."

When she was on the porch, Rutherford smiled. "Ah, the witch from Salem. It is time for your final rewards."

"Leave the boy alone," Josie said.

"Burning you at the stake is my vision," Rutherford shouted. With his staff in one hand and Judgment in the other, he was a frightening sight.

He looked around and laughed. "Rich or poor, we all have our waltz with the Grim Reaper." He turned to Brother Robert. "Torch her."

Laura and Manly came riding up the ravine trail behind the cabin. Brother Robert moved forward but Laura stepped out from the bushes and onto the porch. Manly quietly stood behind her.

"This has got to stop!" Laura shouted.

Rutherford smirked. "This doesn't involve you now. Maybe later, but—"

Manly interrupted. "But maybe nothin'. Time for you to quit this craziness."

Rabbi Stern came to the top of the ridge and looked down. Rutherford and his torchbearers had half-surrounded the house. Josie, Laura, and Manly were on the porch. *Where is Abe? I've got to get to him.*

Judgment's head darted at unseen objects. His tongue poked out toward Laura, making her shiver.

Josie put her hands in front of Laura and Manly. "No need to hurt them or the boy. They ain't done nothin' to you. Your fight's with me. It always has been."

"Josie, no," Laura said.

Josie turned to Laura. "It's all right. I'm just an old woman. You folks got your whole lives ahead."

"Leave my boy alone!" Stern shouted.

"Here I am," Abe shouted weakly, stepping out onto the porch.

Everyone went silent, then Josie stepped in front of him. "Get on back inside, honey. No one's goin' to get you."

Rutherford held the snake over his head. "Judgment, look for the signs. Cleanse us. Bite the evil one."

Rutherford's eyes glistened. His smile was almost trancelike. No one moved as Judgment darted at Manly.

"Manly, no," Laura whispered.

Judgment flew at Manly's face, then at Stern's. His rattling tail was so loud that Abe covered his ears. Judgment came within inches of Stern's face, then reeled back to strike.

"Get the evil one," Rutherford whispered.

The snake turned, moving with lightning speed, and sunk his fangs into Rutherford's neck. Brother Robert cried out, "Nooooooo!"

Rutherford's eyes bulged out and he dropped his staff, but he didn't cry out. Everyone watched his dance of death, as he whirled around, trying to pull the snake off. But it was over before it started. Rutherford was dead.

"I guess he got the evil one," Josie whispered.

Judgment unhooked his fangs and turned away. Laura's horse charged forward and reared up, panicked by the snake. Everyone backed off as the horse stomped the snake's head, then bolted into the woods.

Judgment and Rutherford were dead. Fear came into the Flock's eyes. Brother Robert took the snake in one hand, then lifted Rutherford up. He walked off into the darkness with the Flock following behind.

Stern rushed forward, grabbing Abe into his arms. "Oh, Abe. I was so worried."

"Everything was okay," Abe said. "I was with Josie."

"What's this on your head?" Stern asked.

Abe giggled about the plaid potholder. "It's my Ozark special. Josie gave it to me when I lost my yarmulke."

Stern smiled. "You are quite a woman, Miss Josie."

"Just tryin' to help one of my patients," she said, laughing.

"But you saved my son's life," Stern said.

"And you all probably saved mine," she said.

Rabbi Stern bowed his head. "This has all been a miracle, a mountain miracle."

"Just let me nurse your boy back to health and you can call it anythin' you want," Josie said.

"Whatever you say," Stern smiled. "But I've got something for you." Taking off the Star of David that hung around his neck, he presented it to Josie. "I want you to have this."

"I'll put it with my collection."

"Collection?" Laura asked.

"Right in here." Josie smiled and opened up a cabinet on the porch wall. Inside were crosses, stars, and other religious symbols she'd been given over the years.

"My patients are always tryin' to help me get to heaven. I just laugh and tell 'em that I'll be waitin' for 'em at the gate."

"Is everything okay?" Sheriff Peterson shouted, making his way down the last half of the ridge path.

"The cavalry's arrived in the nick of time," Manly said dryly. He looked at the black bowler the sheriff was wearing. "I like your hat."

Everyone laughed at the sheriff's blush. "Lost mine in the dark when I was knocked off my horse."

"You never know what will happen on Friday the 13th," Laura said, laughing.

CHAPTER 34

FRIDAY THE 13TH

It *was* Friday the 13th, the day Maurice had said was the unluckiest day of all. He had dared the Younguns to walk through the graveyard and touch the rafter where Old Fred had hung himself, and that is what they were determined to do.

"We gotta get out of here," Larry whispered in the hall outside their bedroom. "He dared us to do it."

"You go. He dared you, not me," Terry said.

Larry shook his head. "He dared us all. He dared the family name."

"Then send pa. I don't want to go," Terry said.

"You're comin' or I'll tell Pa about—" Larry paused, enjoying the pressure he was putting on his brother.

"Or you'll tell him what?"

"Let's see," Larry said, scratching his chin. "There are so many things you've done that he don't know about."

"But Mrs. Wrinkles will hear us leavin'," Terry protested.

"Mrs. Winkler's asleep," Sherry said quietly, looking at the old church lady who'd come over to babysit while Rev. Youngun and Carla went buggy riding in the moonlight.

"Why'd they have to go buggy ridin' in the dark anyway," Terry asked.

"Pa said he had some things he wanted to talk to Miss Carla about," Larry answered.

"I hope they're not kissin'," Terry said. "I'd never be able to look at Pa again."

The old church lady snorted loudly from the couch in the parlor. She'd fallen asleep reading Bible stories to the children, which had almost put them to sleep as well.

Beezer the parrot squawked from his dining-room perch. "Say your prayers."

"Cover that stupid bird," Larry said, " 'fore he wakes Mrs. Wrinkle-face up."

"Her name's not Wrinkle-face," Sherry said. "It's Winkler."

"Winkler, tinkler . . . let's wheel," Terry whispered. "We got to go touch Old Fred's rafter . . . 'cause we're the Younguns," he said sarcastically.

So they slipped out into the darkness without a lantern, using just the light of the full moon to guide them.

"It sure is dark," Terry said, looking around.

"Who turned off the moon?" Sherry asked.

"Just clouds passin' by," Larry whispered.

Terry stopped. "Did you hear that noise?" he asked as they edged around the barn.

"What noise?" Sherry asked, hugging Larry's leg.

The three Younguns listened but could only hear their own breathing. Night wrapped around them; the darkness scared them. Listening for sounds, their imaginations ran wild.

They could hear themselves breathing but it sounded like something else. It was as if the closet boogie man of their nightmares had gotten loose.

"I think someone bad is near us," Larry whispered.

Then they all heard it. They heard the footsteps! A wet nose nudged against Sherry's hand and she screamed, "It's got me!"

Bashful the fainting goat fell over.

"Oh no, it's Bashful," Terry said, disgustedly.

"Come on . . . let's get outta here," Larry said.

They left Bashful and headed into town, the three of them riding on the back of Crab Apple the mule. It was Friday the 13th and they'd never sneaked out at night. Every nightmare they'd ever had was coming back, lurking in the shadows.

A slight wind rustled the leaves as they neared the graveyard. They tied up Crab Apple and looked at the gravestones in front of them.

"Do we gotta cross through it?" Terry whispered. His mind was racing with images of ragged figures, dragging chains and moaning after them, pulling them into their holes, never to be seen again.

"Yup . . . that's the dare," Larry whispered.

Ahead of them, the graveyard was covered with strange shadows. As they walked through the rusted gates, a bat flew between them. Sherry screamed and knocked Terry over.

"It was a vampire!" she gasped.

"Just a bat," Terry said, but his imagination was running wild.

"Wonder if Old Fred's hogs are around?" Larry asked.

"If I hear one pig snort, I'm leavin'," Terry announced.

Each step through the graveyard was torture. Each grave seemed just a temporary resting place for someone, something ready to reach out and grab them.

At a freshly dug grave, they stopped. "Who's in there?" Terry asked, looking at the flowers.

"Don't know and don't want to know," Sherry moaned.

"Come on," Larry said. "It's not too much farther."

Up ahead, Old Fred's house awaited them. "Let's go home," Terry said.

"Can't . . . we got dared," Larry said heading toward the house.

"Watch your step," Larry said to Sherry.

"Why?"

" 'Cause you're steppin' on Mr. Simmons—the old man who died last year," Terry said, pointing to the headstone.

They stopped at the metal fence and looked up. The clouds parted and moonlight bathed the house.

"This is the fence where the robber got killed and the hogs ate his guts," Larry said.

Terry fingered the rust. "You can still see the blood."

"That's rust," Larry said, jostling his hair.

"Rusted blood," Sherry said, her eyes wide.

The porch of the old house was littered with trash and old boxes. A black cat was sitting on the rail.

"It's a black cat," Terry whispered.

"That's part of the dare," Larry said, trying to sound brave.

"Well, you go up there and walk in front of him," Terry said. "I'll wait here."

"Scaredy cat," Larry said, inching forward.

"Don't like cats anyway."

The cat jumped down and ran in front of them all. "Oh, great," Terry exclaimed, "now we've all had it. Seven years of bad luck."

Larry climbed up onto the porch. "Watch your step. There's a board missing."

"I don't believe in ghosts anyway," Terry said, then screamed. "Get him off me . . . get the ghost off me!"

A sheet tacked over the broken window had rippled out with the breeze and wrapped around Terry's head.

"It's only a sheet," Larry snickered.

"I knew it all the time," Terry huffed, pulling the sheet off his face.

"What happens if we see Old Fred?" Sherry whispered.

"Say your prayers," Larry said.

Sherry looked at the front door, then knocked.

"What are you doin'?" Terry whispered.

"Just seein' if Old Fred's home," she said.

"Get outta my way," Larry said. The rusty hinges of the front door creaked as Larry pushed against it.

"I don't believe in ghosts . . . I don't believe in ghosts," Terry whispered to himself.

Across town, Rev. Youngun and Carla Pobst were returning from their buggy ride. At the front door of the Mansfield Hotel, he held her hands.

"I had a wonderful evening," he said, looking into her eyes.

"So did I, Thomas."

It was one of those awkward lovers' moments, so finally, Carla leaned up and kissed him lightly on the lips. "I think I love you, Thomas Youngun . . . I really think I do."

"I know I love you," he whispered, kissing her again.

He thought of nothing but the kiss on the ride home. Whistling and singing as he rode along, Rev. Youngun skipped up the porch steps like a young boy.

"Mrs. Winkler—I'm home," he called out.

A loud snort answered him.

Rev. Youngun looked into the parlor. Mrs. Winkler was fast asleep in the easy chair. "Poor old woman," he whispered, "she must be tired."

Tip-toeing up the stairs, he went to check on the children. They were gone!

"Larry, Terry, Sherry . . . come out . . . I'm home . . . quit hiding from me."

But no one answered. Rev. Youngun rushed downstairs and shook the elderly church lady awake. "Mrs. Winkler . . . Mrs. Winkler . . . where are the children?"

"Wha . . . what?" she stammered, still half-asleep.

"The children . . . they're not in their beds . . . did they go someplace?"

She sat up. "They were talking up a storm about the dare that Maurice Springer put on them. I got sick of hearing about Old Fred, so I told them to sit around and listen to Bible stories . . . Guess I fell asleep."

"Old Fred?" Rev. Youngun scratched his head.

"The one who lived behind the cemetery . . . hung by that thief in his attic."

Rev. Youngun went to the kitchen wall phone and had the operator connect him with the Springers. On the eighth ring, he was ready to give up, then Maurice answered.

"Maurice, this is Thomas Youngun, are my kids over there?"

"Over here? No, they ain't."

"Mrs. Winkler says they were talkin' about some dare you gave them and—"

"Dare? Oh, no," Maurice groaned.

"What? What is it, Maurice?"

"It's the 13th."

"So?"

"They were askin' me about witches and I told them the story 'bout Old Fred who got hung in the house behind the graveyard."

"And?"

"I was jokin' and dared them to go into the spooky house on Friday the 13th and touch the rafter where Old Fred was hung."

"You dared them?"

"I told them I was kiddin'."

"You think that's where they are?"

"It's my fault, but yes, I bet that's where they are. I'll come with you."

Rev. Youngun returned to Mrs. Winkler and told her to sleep in Sherry's room until he got back. He didn't notice Dangit slipping out the door.

It took awhile for the Younguns to get their courage up. Terry thought for sure that he'd heard a ghost, so he insisted that they look around every corner on the first floor. He looked behind the abandoned chairs, Sherry in the closets, and Larry under the rugs.

"Are you sure you heard somethin'?" Larry asked.

"Fur sure, cross my heart I heard somethin'."

"When are we goin' up to the attic?" Sherry asked.

"I guess we better get up there," Larry said, looking around.

The wind sent the ragged curtains in the old house flying. At the top of the stairs, Larry paused, signaling for silence. "Did you hear footsteps?"

"Sounded like someone walkin' 'round out on the porch," Terry whispered.

"Maybe it's Old Fred," Sherry shivered.

Then the sound came through the front door, then stopped. "I know I heard it that time," Terry whispered. "Let's get out of here."

Six Youngun eyes went wide as saucers as the scratching sound started toward the stairs. Sherry closed her eyes. "Now I lay me down to sleep, I—"

Terry bopped her. "Quiet . . . it's comin'."

"What's comin'?" she whimpered.

"Dangit, how the heck do I know!"

Hearing his name misused, Dangit leaped up the stairs and grabbed onto Terry's pants legs. Terry screamed, Larry cried out, and Sherry rolled down the stairs.

"It's got me! The vampire's got me!" Terry screamed.

Larry saw who it was in the moonlight. "It's only Dangit."

"Dangit?" Terry exclaimed. "Why, I knew it all the time."

Sherry came back up the stairs, rubbing her head. "Why'd you push me down the stairs, Terry?"

"I didn't."

"Come on," said Larry. "Let's get up to the attic and touch the rafter. I want to be home before Pa gets there."

Maurice and Rev. Youngun pulled up outside the cemetery gates. "I don't see them," Rev. Youngun said.

"They're 'round here somewhere, I just know it."

Then they heard the children cry out from inside the old house. "That's them," Maurice said. "They're in the house."

Another curtain had wrapped around the children as they approached the stairs to the third floor. They all screamed until they managed to crawl out from what they thought was a ghost.

Halfway up the third floor stairs, Terry held up his hand. "Somethin's in the air."

Larry listened. "I don't hear anythin'."

Terry shook his head. "Not a noise . . . a smell . . . see?"

Larry sniffed and scrunched his nose at the awful smell. "What's that?" he asked.

"Think it's a ghost?" Terry whispered, smelling it again.

Larry held his nose. "A ghost smell? What kind of ghost is that?"

" 'Cuse me," Sherry blushed.

Terry bopped her and headed up the stairs. Then they heard footsteps enter the house. Real footsteps. They didn't know it was their father and Maurice. They thought it was Old Fred.

"Fred's comin'!" Larry screamed, racing up the stairs. Terry and Sherry came right behind. They rounded the corner on the third floor and took the stairs, two at a time to the attic.

"Come down here," came a voice muffled by the three floors in between.

"Oh no," Terry moaned, "it's Fred . . . he's come back."

"Can't be," Larry whispered.

They heard the footsteps coming up to the second floor.

"Sounds like Old Fred's brought a ghost friend with him." Sherry shivered.

"What are we goin' to do?" Terry asked.

"Let's get somethin' to defend ourselves with," Larry said. He picked up an old chair leg. "Somethin' like this."

"What good will that do?" Terry asked. "Ghosts are thin air."

"Maybe, maybe not," Larry said.

Rev. Youngun looked around the second floor but didn't see the children. "Maybe they're not here," he said.

Maurice shook his head. "I know I heard 'em."

Then Dangit came up, wagging his tail.

"Where are they, boy?" Rev. Youngun asked.

Dangit started up the stairs. "I bet they're in the attic," Maurice said, following behind.

At the foot of the attic stairs, Maurice called out, "You kids up there?"

"Who's askin'?" Larry shouted back.

"Me . . . Maurice and your daddy."

Larry looked at his brother and sister. Terry whispered, "Probably a ghost trick."

"Go away, Fred . . . go away, ghost man," Terry shouted.

Maurice shrugged and started up the stairs. The Younguns crawled in different directions, trying to find hiding places. Terry tried hiding behind an old trunk but saw a shelf on top of the big hangman's rafter and climbed up and hid.

"Come on, kids . . . I was just kiddin' with the dare . . . that's all," Maurice said.

When he stuck his head above the attic floor, Larry breathed a sigh of relief. "Mr. Springer . . . it's you."

"Who else would be fool enough to come lookin' for you kids in this old house?"

Rev. Youngun looked over the edge. "Come on, children. It's time to go home to bed."

Sherry ran into his arms. Larry shrugged. "We just wanted to do what you dared us to do."

Maurice nodded. "I know. Guess I shouldn't be kiddin' with you children so much."

"Is it true that Old Fred hid his gold somewhere in the house?" Terry asked, sitting on the rafter. He reached over toward an object in the corner of the rafter.

Rev. Youngun shook his head. "That's just an old tale . . . nothin' but hokum."

"That's right," Maurice nodded, "just a tall tale."

Terry looked at what was in his hand, holding it up to the fractured moonlight. "Then what's this?" he asked, flipping the coin he found to Maurice.

"It's gold! It's a fifty-dollar gold coin!" Maurice exclaimed.

CHAPTER 35

NEW BEGINNINGS

The next morning, Maurice told about Terry finding the gold coin to Hambone, who told Mom, who told Otis, who told just about everybody in town. By noontime, the sheriff had to post a deputy at the house to keep the looters out.

Terry gave the gold coin to his father to hold, who immediately informed him that he'd save it for Terry's college education. "I can kiss that coin good-bye," Terry grumbled.

"But it's for your college," his father protested.

"I want to go to candy college. Don't need money—just good teeth and a big appetite."

When the sheriff went to check on the Flock at the old Williams place, he found it deserted. They'd taken all their belongings. Rutherford's body was nowhere to be found.

The only thing they left was Bill Ponder in his grave. Susan and her children went back to the barn to stand by her husband's grave and found Josie kneeling there.

"What you folks goin' to do?" Josie asked.

Susan turned. "I don't know. I hate leavin' Bill up here by himself and don't have much to go back to in Georgia."

"I don't got much . . . just a small cabin. But I got some good land and a garden."

Susan wasn't sure what Josie was saying. "I don't understand."

Josie cleared her throat. "I'm sayin' that if you and the little ones need a place to stay for a bit, well, you're welcome."

A tear slid down Susan's cheek. "Will you teach me about herbs . . . and helpin' people?"

"If you're willin' to learn, why, I'll introduce you to Mother Nature herself!" Josie was so excited that she took the children by the hand and danced along the path. Susan followed behind smiling.

Leaving their things at the cabin, they went to town for the Founder's Day celebration. Josie even took out the last store-bought dress she had—which she remembered purchasing in 1892.

Mansfield was decked out for the Founder's Day events. It was like a small Fourth of July celebration, without the fireworks.

Carla Pobst had left on the morning train for Cape Girardeau, Missouri, promising to return soon. They'd finally talked about marriage, but both wanted to think about it some more.

Sarah Bentley was in the spotlight, directing where the chairs should be put and how the food should be displayed.

"In New York, we'd do it this way," she said to Hambone, who was laying out a spread of food.

"And in Missouri, we do it this way," he said, putting a deviled egg into his mouth and swallowing it in one bite.

From the podium, Sarah Bentley tried to make an inspiring speech about teamwork and dedication, but it largely fell on deaf ears. The kids just wanted to hear the starter's gun to begin the race.

It was during the prerace speeches that Terry made his first buck selling treasure maps. He had a good thing going for about an hour, until his father got wind of his enterprise. Though he made him promise that he wouldn't make any more maps, Terry didn't tell him about the three in his pocket, so he managed to pick up three more quarters before the race.

Larry and Sherry had their regular shoes on, but Terry looked down. He still had his old shoes on. He adjusted the visor of his baseball cap.

Josie saw Terry standing there and pulled out a pair of shoes from her carrying sack.

"What are you doing?" Susan asked.

Josie smiled. "Got some old business to finish up. Here's a quarter. You take the kids and buy 'em some candy."

Dangling the shoes behind her back, Josie walked over to Terry. "Hey, Red."

Terry turned. It was Josie. "What do you want?" he asked.

"Got your shoes like I promised."

Terry's eyes brightened. "You do? Gosh, I need 'em for the race. These are so small that my toes are touching my heel."

"Well, put these on," she smiled, handing him back his shoes.

"Gosh, I thought you gave 'em to that old man."

Josie shook her head. "If you hadn't run off so fast, I'd have given 'em back to you that night."

Terry took off his old shoes and handed them to Josie. "What are these for?" she laughed.

"For your tree," he smiled. "Maybe some poor person could use 'em."

"Maybe I put a good hex on you after all," she winked.

"Naw . . . just don't like to have extra shoes around. Pa's always tryin' to get me to polish 'em like I was in the army or somethin'."

"Think you're goin' to win the race?" Josie asked.

"If I had your broom, I could win in nothin' flat."

Josie shook her head. "Still thinkin' I'm a witch, eh?"

"Don't know what to believe . . . except that I want to thank you for savin' my friend Abe."

"So you heard?" Josie said.

"Everyone's heard . . . you're a hero."

"And you're a little treasure hunter I hear . . . sellin' treasure maps like this," she said, pulling out a map.

"Where'd you get that?" he asked.

"Bought it from the baker's son . . . he also told me you sold him some of my witch's broom straw . . . is that so?"

Terry shrugged. "Boy's got to earn his candy money, don't he?"

Josie laughed. "You're all right, Red. Here's a nickel."

"Gosh, thanks, Josie!" He looked over and saw Abe walking with his father, "Hey, there's Abe. See ya."

Terry ran over. "Hi, Terry," Abe said.

"You goin' to race?" Terry asked.

Abe shrugged. "Can't. Maybe next year."

Rabbi Stern patted Terry on the head. "You boys be good. I go talk to some of our new neighbors."

Laura and Manly walked over and looked at Abe. "How're you feeling?" she asked.

Abe smiled. "Eatin' my grass and garlic . . . just like Doctor Josie ordered."

"Don't eat too much garlic or you'll be seein' Dr. George." Manly smiled.

"Josie's working with Dr. George to make me well."

"Then you're in four good hands," Manly said. "Excuse me, Laura, but I want to go talk with the sheriff a moment."

Laura turned to Abe. "Next year you'll be racing," she smiled, walking off.

Abe and Terry headed over to the starting line. "Wish me luck," said Terry.

"Luck," smiled Abe.

"Don't lose your yamiwhatsit," Terry laughed, tapping the black skullcap that Abe's father had given him to replace the one that was lost.

"Help . . . help!" a woman shouted.

Everyone turned. A horse with a papoose style baby carrier strapped on was racing toward the starting line.

Sarah Bentley cried out, "Children, get out of the way!"

Everyone scattered except Terry and Abe.

"My baby, help, my baby!" the frantic woman shouted, running after the horse.

Rabbi Stern came out from Bedal's General Store. "Abe, get out of the way!"

No one knew what went through the two boys' heads, but they both went running toward the horse with their hands up.

Rev. Youngun saw what was happening and scrambled through the crowd. "Terry . . . get out of the way . . . you'll get killed."

"Whoa," Terry said to the horse, but the horse didn't stop.

Abe shouted, "Stop!"

The horse kept coming at full speed toward them. People covered their eyes, not wanting to see the boys get run over.

Terry and Abe stood their ground, hand in hand, blocking the horse's path. Abe didn't even notice that his yarmulke had fallen off his head and was trampled by the crowd in all the excitement.

At the last moment, the horse reared up in front of them. With his hoofs punching the air, the horse came down snorting. Terry grabbed the reins and kept the horse steady, while Abe climbed up and got the crying baby off.

"My baby . . . my baby!" the mother cried. "Oh, thank you for saving my baby," she said, as Abe handed the screaming child to her. She looked at both boys and said, "It was a miracle . . . you both saved my baby."

"It was nothin'," Terry shrugged. "We do it all the time."

Abe giggled as they were surrounded by the other kids, slapping them on the back. Terry noticed Abe's bare head and went into Bedal's General Store.

"What can I do for you, Terry?" Lafayette Bedal asked.

"Can I borrow your scissors?"

After cutting the visor off his hat, Terry walked out and handed it to Abe. "What's that?" Abe asked.

"It's a yami special," Terry smiled, "made in Missouri. You got to keep your head covered, don't ya?"

Abe laughed and put it on his head. "You're my best friend, Terry."

"Just hold onto your yami . . . I don't have anymore baseball caps with me."

On the podium, Rabbi Stern handed Laura a folded piece of paper. "What is it?" she asked.

"Open it," the Rabbi smiled.

Laura unfolded the paper. It was the front page of Rabbi Stern's first newspaper, printed in Yiddish.

"What does the headline say?" Laura asked.

Stern took a deep breath, then read the headline in Yiddish. "What do you think?" he asked proudly.

Laura laughed. "What does it say?"

Stern blushed. "I'm sorry. I thought everyone spoke the mother tongue. It says 'America is the promised land'."

"It certainly is," Laura said.

Stern saw Lafayette Bedal waving him over toward his general store. "Excuse me, Laura."

Susan Ponder came up with Josie. "Guess what, Laura?" Josie said.

"What?" Laura said.

"Susan and her children are going to move in with me. She wants to learn the healin' art of herb medicine."

"That's wonderful!" Laura exclaimed.

Susan smiled. "I've heard and seen so much bad that I want to spend my time helping people."

"Be a bit crowded in your cabin, won't it, Josie?"

"I haven't told her yet, but we're goin' to add on some bedrooms and put in a place for my patients. It'll be like havin' a family of my own," Josie grinned.

Laura smiled and looked over the people of Mansfield. The town had a new rabbi, some new residents, and a new attitude.

People were stopping to talk with Josie, accepting her as a friend and neighbor. Rabbi Stern had found that America was indeed the land of promise and had come out of his self-imposed shell.

The witch talk was dead and the Flock had left in the night, taking Rutherford's body with them. Judgment was left for the vultures in the crook of the lightning tree. The old Williams place was abandoned once again, except for Bill Ponder, whose grave served as a reminder of what can happen when people close their minds to reason.

The starter gun sounded and the children took off. The next generation of Mansfield raced down the street, each hoping to win the prize.

But the real prize was won by everyone—they'd won the prize of new beginnings. A time to start fresh, forgive and forget, shake hands, and agree to be friends.

It was a time for the healing in the hearts and attitudes of the people of Mansfield. Friends instead of strangers. Reason instead of superstition. Caring instead of turning away.

People helping people—that was the true mountain miracle that happened in Mansfield.

ABOUT THE AUTHOR

T. L. Tedrow is a best-selling author, screenwriter, and film producer. His books include the eight-book Days of Laura Ingalls Wilder series, *Missouri Homestead, Children of Promise, Good Neighbors, Home to the Prairie, The World's Fair, Mountain Miracle, The Great Debate,* and *Land of Promise,* which are the basis for a new television series. His upcoming eight-book series, *The Younguns,* has also been sold as a television series. His first best-seller, *Death at Chappaquiddick,* has been made into a feature film. He lives with his wife, Carla, and their four children in Winter Park, Florida.